LURES

A collection of short stories and poems

ALSO BY JOHN DIFELICE

American Zeroes

LURES

Careful What You Fish For

JOHN DIFELICE

LURES

Copyright © 2017 by John DiFelice

All short stories and poems written by John DiFelice.

"Stan Slade and the Case of the Killer Meme" was originally published in the short story collection "South Philly Fiction," Don Ron Books, 2013.

Printed in the United States of America

First Printing, 2017

ISBN-13: 978-1537129280
ISBN-10: 1537129287

www.johndifelice.com

For Leo

Contents

Swallow me
Like Alice did
And Neo's choice
That wasn't his
Drink from a cup
Or use a dish
Tadpole size
From Jonah's fish
And when at last
The time has come
Smile sweetly
My dear one

DOES THE WORLD MAKE SENSE?

CHRISTIANS WILL TELL YOU that we all have our crosses to bear in life. For some it's disease or loneliness, for others it's being born without any discernible talent or reason for existing. For Ernie Pendleton, it was his plastic bathtub-shower combo, a piece of engineering feculence so poorly wrought and installed that it made a high-pitched gasp every time he stepped on a spot in the center of the basin. What made this sound unfortunate—unfortunate for Ernie—is that when it was filtered through the three layers of polyurethane that covered his oak flooring, and then passed through the space between the bathroom subfloor and the living room ceiling thick with plaster and lath, it emerged as the moan of a woman nearing orgasm.

This alone would not have been tantamount to Ernie dragging a wooden crossbeam to the summit of a hill where he would be nailed to it and hoisted, naked, to the mockery of all. To understand the comparison, one would have to understand Ernie's wife, Dora, and how at any point in the day she became convinced that Ernie was having an affair.

Ernie was not an unpleasant-looking man, but he was not what people would call handsome either. Despite this, a typical morning in Ernie's life included waking alone in his bed to the smells of Dora making coffee downstairs, putting on slippers that were a few loose threads from disintegrating, taking the short walk in his slippers to the edge of the bathtub-shower combo, removing them along with whatever passed for his pajamas the night before (which were often the clothes he wore to the office the day before), turning on the warm shower, and then stepping into it with a nameless apprehension. He always washed his face first, during which time his eyes and mouth would be tightly closed, and he would invariably step backward onto the spot that made the sound that caused the loss of water pressure as the kitchen sink faucet opened full blast, followed by the sounds of the freezer door swinging open and then slamming shut, followed by the sounds of hurried footsteps on the staircase, the opening of the bedroom door, and the creaks of the floor as forceful and determined footsteps made their advance to the shower where Ernie stood naked. Ernie would brace himself for what came next: the bucket of ice water she dumped onto his head along with the words, "That's for you and your hussy!" before stomping off into the remainder of her morning.

When Ernie described her behavior to friends, they would all say the same thing.

"Why don't you leave her?"

"You know that kind of thing is not normal."

"Why do you put up with her?"

"She loves me," Ernie would reply.

They each would say a variation of "if she loved you she would trust you" and then stop before stating the most obvious point of all: she was all Ernie had because no other woman would have him.

"You know she's crazy," his best friend told him. "Her behavior doesn't make sense."

"Well, does the world make sense?" Ernie asked.

When a marriage is opened and laid flat for others to pick apart and analyze, the meaningful parts collapse and are lost. Ernie knew something none of his friends knew, but something Dora had somehow always known: Ernie lusted after every woman he saw. He never did anything about it, never pursued another women and wouldn't have known how to do it had he had the unlikely opportunity. But he salivated over women at the local food co-op; he discreetly leered at women on the train; he fantasized about the dispossessed Mexican women on the cleaning crews who began their shifts as he was leaving to go home; he stared longingly at the kind, brown-eyed face behind the counter of the Starbucks in his building; he imagined making passionate love to the guilty-looking Asian woman in her Mazda 3 hatchback as she took shallow drags off a cigarette. He wanted them all, and fantasized about them so intensely that he felt he had been unfaithful to his wife. In his mind, she was justified in dumping as many buckets of ice water on him as she pleased. There were not enough buckets of ice water in the world to atone for his betrayal.

On the morning of March fifth, Ernie stepped on the special spot in the tub, heard the usual filling of the bucket, the slamming of the freezer door, the feet stomping up the stairs, the swish of air as the bedroom door opened abruptly, and the freezing cold water and ice that cascaded down over his shoulders and onto his back and legs.

"You better not come home with another woman

on you," she said.

Ernie blamed her threats on his self-diagnosed sexual addiction. Several months back when he had sought a doctor who specialized in such things, the doctor asked him about the frequency and type of his sexual activity. When Ernie said truthfully that he was having no sex at all, the doctor gave him the phone number of a psychiatrist and wished him the best.

Seeing little hope from the medical establishment, Ernie decided that the best way to cure his lust was to avoid all eye contact with women. If he didn't see women, he reasoned, then he couldn't lust after them. He thought of how great it would be if there was a law that required all women to keep their faces hidden, but in the end he felt that such an idea was the height of selfishness.

Ernie had perfect vision, so he bought a pair of powerful reading glasses on March fifth to blur his far sight. It worked flawlessly. When wearing the glasses, he was able to see enough to avoid walking into walls or stop signs, but could not make out any details in a human face. He could barely tell the genders apart, which did result in one embarrassing misunderstanding. A small price to pay, he thought, to shower with confidence.

Everyone at work told him they loved his glasses. He looked like a new man, they said. Halfway through his day, a calm set in that he had never felt before. He did not feel overpowering urges that would cause him to stray from his marriage vows. He no longer felt the need to ogle young women on the company dime. The source of his addiction had finally been removed, and by the cheapest of all means:

ten dollar reading glasses had been his salvation.

Ernie walked the three blocks to his outbound train on the regional rail line on March Fifth. The air had a hint of sweetness, like from old wood in a confessional where his carnal sins had been absolved. He cautiously navigated the escalator and stairs leading down to his train platform. He couldn't see anything and he was happy. Had he been able to see more than six inches in front of his face, he might have noticed the suspicious-looking woman with the baby carriage that held no baby. A flash and a sonic boom later, and Ernie was covered with her. The train pulling into the station had taken most of the blast which cut a deep hole into it and blew the car from its tracks. Ernie staggered around in a daze amid the substantial casualties, eyes wide opened, vision fully restored because the blast had blown the glasses off of his face. He looked down at himself and saw that he was covered with another woman. He heard the last thing his wife had said to him before he left for work.

Ernie took a cab home to avoid the ensuing chaos of police sirens, ambulances, reporters, and rubberneckers. The cab driver was too drunk to notice his appearance and didn't ask questions. When Ernie arrived home he went straight to his bedroom shower and undressed. He stepped into the bathtub-shower combo, but did not turn on the water. He stood under the shower nozzle and took a deep breath. But when he meant to exhale, what came out instead was a prolonged sob, followed by another, and another, and another. He cupped his face with his hands and felt his knees shake. He stepped back onto the spot that created the moan. He heard the kitchen faucet turned on full blast; he heard the footsteps on the stairs, he heard the bedroom door open. He braced himself for his punishment, for the water torture he had come to expect, but the water wasn't cold. It was warm. The water washed the filth and gore from his hair and body. Ernie turned on the water to the shower and stood under it with his eyes squeezed shut, not wanting to open them until the water was clear, until he was clean.

Later that night, Ernie sat on the sofa with his arm around Dora and watched the news coverage of the train bombing. They watched the profiles of the victims, the heartbreaking details of lives cut short. Dora put her hand on Ernie's knee, something she had not done in so long that Ernie could not remember when. He turned to face her as the news anchors put forth theories of who was responsible for the attack. He smiled at her and she smiled back. They held the gaze for a time until her eyes narrowed and her smile fell as she spoke.

"You're lucky that wasn't perfume."

THAT SOUND

Do you hear that sound?
What sound?
Never mind
Do you hear that sound?
What sound?
That one
No, I don't hear
the sound that's like
a kettle drum
a baby's cry
an old man's moan
as he slowly dies
boughs rubbing themselves raw
in winds howling
between buildings that
scrape the sky
I don't hear that sound
Me neither
It was my heart
pounding all this time

ICH GROLLE NICHT

MY WIFE SARAH AND I sit in the doctor's office in front of a large mahogany desk. It looks like a desk belonging to a serious man who does serious deeds. Upon his walls hang citations and framed magazine covers that praise his brilliance at joining seed to egg in such a way that it very often results in the birth of a human baby. No alien DNA here, that would be cheating. The thought of alien DNA, in addition to its inherent coolness, is a fine example of how my mind copes with stress. Whenever I'm in a stressful situation, like awaiting the latest results in a series of disappointing fertility tests, my mind wanders far into the absurd. I envision Grey Aliens impregnating my wife as they deride me for failing at my one biological duty and sole reason for existing on earth. The aliens are short and bald and smell like cheese. What Sarah and I have gone through over the past year to get pregnant is as alien to me as this extraterrestrial vision, and nearly as unromantic. It certainly does not match the blessed expectations of conception that my parents had drilled into my head, right after they stopped scaring the shit out of me with tales of unwanted pregnancies and right before they started bugging me for grandkids. I have always imagined the act of conception as the very height of romance, complete with mood lighting and Hungarian Dance playing in the background.

Our names are spoken abruptly by a man standing in the doorway. It is a serious voice that snaps me out of my other-worldly reverie, a rich baritone that would be perfect for Schumann's "Ich Grolle Nicht" or other art songs. *Ich grolle nicht, und wenn das Herz auch bricht.* Roughly translated: I bear no grudge, even though my heart is breaking.

We had decided that it was time for a new fertility doctor, and the man we are meeting is supposedly the best. He walks into his own office and sits down in his command chair across the desk from us. He is really short, which I note because his voice does not match his stature. Despite this, he is what I guess women would consider handsome, and has a powerful presence designed to win respect quickly. He has intelligent eyes, a full head of black hair, and very muscular arms. He wears scrubs like he was born into them, and his black chest hair pops from the v-neck of his scrubs unapologetically, reveling in its hairy, retro-style virility. My eyes cut to his eyes, then to his muscles, then to his chest hair, back to his eyes, to his head, to the Grey Aliens, back to his chest hair, to the orchestra playing Hungarian Dance, to his chest hair, and then to the door through which we can make a dash. Ultimately my eyes come to rest on Sarah who sits quietly awaiting the results of our tests. Her smile is soft and her face warm and hopeful. Her large brown eyes look at me and then narrow into a little squint that raises the corners of my mouth. I fell in love with that face. She would make such a great mom. I know how anxious she has been about our meeting with the doctor, and the least I can do is control my thoughts and keep them positive. I have as much at stake as Sarah does, maybe even more. I donated a lot of sperm for this test.

"Let's not waste each other's time, shall we?" he says. That doesn't sound good. Sarah shoots me a glance, her eyes already filled with anxiety. "With fertility, as with comedy," he continues, "timing is everything."

He pauses for what seems like too long and then lets out a booming laugh that startles me. But Sarah laughs with him. I turn to see a look of relief on her face. He must've sensed her tension and thought to make her relax with an icebreaker joke. Maybe this man is as good as all the magazine covers say he is. If that's the case, then I should be smiling too.

I laugh, but by the time I do it sounds out of place. The time to laugh has passed. Is this the comedic timing he spoke of?

"Now," he begins with a controlled intensity. "Here's what we know." He lowers his voice so we'll lean in close. The bush on his chest seems to increase as he speaks, the hairs multiplying with the promise of our own fertility. "We're going to be upfront and honest with each other," he says. "There's no point in sugar-coating things. That would be a waste of your time, and of my time. Understand?" Sarah is nodding her head in complete agreement. She's all in.

He tells me that my sperm have good motility (good swimmers) and good morphology (won't be featured as circus geeks), but that there are too few of them. The doctor adds, "You're playing in an arena, my friend, for a crowd of one hundred." That inspired me to join in the fun. I crack a joke of my own, but there is silence except for the buzzing of the doctor's cell phone. Sarah gives me her "you're killing me softly" look, and the doctor becomes stone-faced, all traces of humor gone from his once jovial expression.

"This is a very serious matter," he lectures me. "It is not a time for levity, and we never use slang when speaking about reproductive material. Please use the proper terminology to show some respect for what I do, or don't talk about it at all."

I apologize to him in a stunned sort of way. He turns to Sarah.

"Naturally," he says, "I will play an important role in your artificial insemination." He turns to me. "Mainly, my job is to make sure your wife doesn't bring a big blonde guy with her to mix his in." His laugh rings out and bounces around the small room. I look at Sarah for some acknowledgement that she heard it too, but her mind is somewhere else, probably planning her baby shower. I wish my mind could be anywhere else.

Ich grolle nicht.

As we shake goodbye, he tries in earnest to break every finger and metacarpal in my right hand.

"Come back next Tuesday, and let's see if I can knock up your wife." He laughs again and slaps me on the back really hard and sends us on our way.

Sarah is silent in the passenger seat as I pull out of the hospital parking lot.

"Can that guy try any harder to be macho?" I ask, once I think we are a sufficient distance from the hospital, as if he could somehow hear us.

"I thought he was nice," she says.

"Really? Did you hear what he said to me? Where did that guy learn his bedside manner? You want to deal with him for who knows how many months?"

"All I care about is that he's good at what he does. He can tell as many bad jokes as he wants, so long as we get pregnant. Right?" Sarah has become very pragmatic during this whole baby-making process.

What Sarah doesn't appreciate is that I will be interacting with him much more than she will. I will have to make several deposits of semen so they can be spun in a centrifuge to make one good, concentrated batch. That means lots of quality time in Dr. Sperm's lavatory for me.

I say "Dr. Sperm's lavatory" for two reasons.

First, I have nicknamed him Dr. Sperm because my main interaction with him will be handing him cups of my genetic material. Second, I have already decided that I will produce the semen samples only at the clinic. I don't want to do it at home, even though it means doing it in a bright, stark hospital bathroom with people waiting outside who know exactly what I am doing inside. But it is better than doing it at home. At home would be all wrong. It is bad enough that I've had scheduled sex with my wife for the past year; having scheduled sex with myself in my own house is too weird to consider seriously. I also feel that as a general rule, freshness matters, plus it will eliminate the chance of something terrible happening, like getting into a car accident on the way to the doctor's office and police finding me walking around dazed and covered with my own sample. Would they believe I had done the deed at home and was simply delivering the semen to our fertility doctor? Surely they would want to know how the accident happened. They would interrogate me under a 120 watt bulb and deny me a moist towelette. The headline "Man crashes while masturbating in car" flashes before my eyes for an awful split second. Not for this man. No, this man will be safe within the confines of the white, tiled walls of Dr. Sperm's bathroom. It's like anything else in life: you pick your indignity and move on.

      I complain about Dr. Sperm all the way home until Sarah tells me to shut up. I devise a million retorts to his jokes that I should've said at the time until I feel that I've somehow redeemed myself. Then something strange happens. I begin to empathize with Dr. Sperm. I being to think that maybe I have judged him too harshly. Maybe there is a reason for his attempts to inject humor into the process, no matter how misplaced. Within the myriad sob stories and desperate pleas, maybe he has lost sight of the humanity in his art. I can hardly blame him for that. He can't dwell anymore on our particular misfortune as any other. All of his patients are deserving. Doctors need some distance between themselves and their patients. Without it, Dr. Sperm might empathize with us too much. He might hear what remains unspoken in our house, of lifting the toilet lid for the nth consecutive month and seeing the diffuse reddish tint that tells me we'll have to try again. Next month will be the one, next month for sure. The color red becomes the enemy, the sign of further disappointment in our attempts to have a child. It becomes the color of heartbreak. The doctor would have to walk down the steps with me to where Sarah stands in the kitchen, walk up behind her, gently place his arms around her, and tell her that it will be ok and that he loves her, all without saying a word. He would have to hear the sounds of a house filled with children as the pitch bends and drops as they move away from us, farther and farther into the dark distance until the sounds disappear completely. He'd have to see the lights in each bedroom, each one where a child would sleep—each the sole justification for buying a home with more rooms than Sarah and I would ever need—and then watch them go out one by one. The tiny socks and shoes, gone. The toys from birthdays that never came. Everything slipping into an uncertain, lonely future.

Months pass as I am ambushed by horrible thoughts, ones I must forever keep to myself. I envision the family I could have if only I had married someone else. I see the face I fell in love with become pixelated as I gaze at it too closely, deconstructing it, stripping it down to its base, genetic components. I fight the thought and I win; it dies, but not before it infects me.

Through all of this I perform my many clandestine, lunchtime trips to the fertility clinic to "do the deed," as I've taken to calling it, with pornographic magazines I'd never buy in a store without wearing a disguise. The sessions are taking longer, each one longer than the one before. I can't feel anything anymore. I need more stimulation. A month later they put a TV and DVD player in the room. I pop a DVD into the player. I'm embarrassed to say I've seen this one.

Each time I slink out of the bathroom I see Dr. Sperm walking down the hallway in his light blue scrubs.

"Hey, no Big Blondie last month." He gives me a thumbs up. I can't think of any one of those million retorts.

Another month comes and goes. Sarah and I have ceased having sex to save my sperm for the inseminations. The doctor said this isn't necessary, that one week of abstinence is enough, but I don't want to take any chances. Sarah was four days late last month and we celebrated too early. We don't want to do that again.

Surprise, there's blood in the toilet, so it's back to Dr. Sperm's. I've decided to shake things up a bit. Today I choose to watch a fortyish social studies teacher instruct her ingénue about the ways of the natives of Lesbos. I have a meeting in an hour about the fee schedules for unified managed accounts and I can't concentrate. I walk out of the room forty minutes later with my cup. I hear a deep voice crack another joke that now seems filled with malice.

At home, things seem fine, but they are not. Sarah and I both have fertility problems, but I find myself thinking about how hers are worse than mine. The doctor can compensate for my problem, but little can be done about hers, making it the chief culprit of our conception troubles. Lately, that's all I can think about when I look at her, that it's more her fault than mine. I don't want to have this thought, but I do.

More red, more porn, more samples, more jokes from Dr. Sperm, more Dr. Sperm trying to crush my hand.

I'm not sure how many more rounds of artificial insemination I can handle. It's expensive, it's time-consuming, and I'm having less sex than ever, which is completely counterintuitive considering that we're trying to have a child. Even masturbation has taken a nose dive since I only do it once a month for the sample. Worse, the whole thing seems pointless and has propelled me into existential despair.

That's why I've decided today will be my last session. Maybe it's the lack of positive results, or maybe it's the inappropriate remarks and jokes from my doctor, but I suddenly feel that this is all Dr. Sperm's fault. He is supposed to be the best, but instead of getting Sarah pregnant, all he did was hone is standup comedy act at my expense.

I know what's going to happen now: I'm going to walk out of here with my cup, and Dr. Sperm is going to walk toward me, chest hair popping out of his scrubs, with his perfect smile and perfect hair and perfectly tanned skin, as he nods to his nurses and patients and prepares to emasculate me with a well-timed zinger. I think it's time to find out if he really has a sense of humor after all. Right after I finish washing my hands, I put a dime-sized dab of soft soap in the center of my palm.

I know what I'm about to do is childish. It is probably the most childish thing I've ever done, even more than when I was five and convinced Richie Harvey that his mom's anus was the Sarlacc Pit on Tatooine, and he had to send in his Jedi Luke Skywalker action figure to kill it. My justification is that since having a child has become my single-minded obsession, and the word "childish" contains the word "child," doing something childish is inherently good.

I walk out of the bathroom and down the hall with a confidence I haven't felt since this whole artificial insemination thing started. Dr. Sperm walks toward me, teeth glistening, chest hair teasing the v-neck of his shirt, right hand clenching as a warm up to our handshake. I walk toward him, grinning ear to ear, with my Soft Soap hand extended. He approaches and grabs my hand and squeezes. There is a pause. He looks at me, then down at our joined hands, and then back at me again without changing his facial expression. I look at him, feign surprise and say, "Oh. Sorry."

I had anticipated two reactions to my little prank. In the first one, Dr. Sperm really does have a sense of humor and we both have a good ole laugh about it.

In the second one, he completely ignores it, resulting in a situation that would be stupendously awkward.

I didn't anticipate how he would really react.

He turned to the people in the waiting room and held out his hand.

"You see, this is why I tell people to make sure they wash their hands after producing a semen sample. Can everyone see this? Hygiene is very important here."

A gasp went up from the room and Dr. Sperm walked away to wash his hands.

I thought I could play a trick on him, but I was wrong. There are those who can prank other people, and those who are pranked, and there's nothing in between. It's all been one big trick on me. How can I not get my wife pregnant? It violates everything about being a man. It's like forgetting how to breath. What's wrong with me? What in God's name is wrong with me?

I arrive home, eat dinner, and go straight to bed. Sarah and I say nothing to each other because there's nothing to say.

I soon find myself asleep and in a strange dream. It is autumn and the weather has just turned. It's getting cold. Any hint of youth has gone out of my face. My skin is ruddy yet fragile, and my body aches all over from the arthritis that invaded my spine and joints. Sarah lies next to me. Her long brown hair and figure that once made me drive nine hours to see her are long ago memories. Her presence now holds the more valuable feelings of comfort and security: the warmth of her body, the chill of her feet pressed against my legs and how they draw warmth from me. Our aged bodies fit together perfectly, molded into our shapes by time and pressure. We are happy, our lives lack nothing because we have each other. All of the fears of growing old childless have passed into that space between a fearful dream and the waking realization of safety.

As I lie next to Sarah and drift into a mixture of past and present, I hear a voice, deep and low, a powerful baritone that calls to me by name. It is accompanied by music, a song I used to know. It is in German.

"Ich Grolle Nicht!"

It's true, I bear no grudge. I am perfectly happy. Society tried to convince us that we had to have a child to be happy, but we proved society wrong. We have led a rich and rewarding life without children. We've traveled the world, we've dined lavishly, we've taken language classes together, we've been involved with a local theater and performed charitable works. We've never had to worry about baby-sitters or cleaning diapers. We haven't spent years of our lives preventing other human beings from committing suicide on a daily basis by drowning, drinking pipe cleaner, electrocution, or jumping out a window because they think they're Word Girl.

I want to stay where I am, but the voice will not allow it. I rise from the bed without waking Sarah, and I notice that I do so without pain. I stand straight and tall, like I did in my youth. I follow the voice out of my front door. I do not feel the cold. I feel nothing but warmth and an anticipation that something new and great is about to happen.

There is light streaming from the other side of the house. I follow it and turn the corner. The music crescendos.

"Ich grolle nicht, und wenn das Herz auch bricht!"

In the middle of my side-mulch bed there is a burning chrysanthemum. Above it hovers a blinding light. When I shield the glare, I can make out golden hairs, more numerous than the stars, popping from a glowing chest under a v-neck scrub shirt.

"Abraham!" the voice booms. "Let's see if we can knock up your wife!"

"Sarah is ninety years-old," I shout. "You couldn't knock her up when she was in her thirties."

He laughs a righteous laugh. "Was it my fault you have the Bill Buckner of testicles between your legs?"

Ouch.

"I can impregnate anyone!" the voice booms.

"How?"

"I mix in my own divine seed! Your son will have a flowing mane of chest hair, and a lucrative career as a jockey!"

I wake. It is morning and Sarah is not in bed. I hear the toilet flush. I prop myself up on my elbow. She turns the corner and looks like she's been crying.

"Is everything all right?" I ask.

"Yes," she says through a sob. "Abe, I have a surprise for you."

"What?"

She holds up something which I can't make out initially. Instead I focus on her face: it is a look of joy and relief, but mostly joy. I look to what she holds in her hand. It's a pregnancy test.

"It's positive," she says, through a giggle.

"Really?" I say. "But how?"

"I guess the man really is a genius."

Genius? This is almost too much to bear. But then it sinks in. We're having a baby. This is not a dream, this is not a construct of my imagination. This is the single greatest moment of my life. "Oh, Sarah!" I exclaim, and run to her. I grab her and hold her and swing her around the small space near our bed.

"Thank you, Abe, for going through this with me...you know, all the treatments. You didn't mind too much, did you?"

I don't know if she realizes what an excellent question that is. I used to think that nothing could ever take the fun out of masturbating. Turns out I was right.

"There's one last thing I want you to do, Abe."

"What?"

"If I tell you what it is, will you promise to do it?"

"Yes." There is nothing I wouldn't do for her.

Sarah tells me to go back to Dr. Sperm's office with a gift and a card and thank him for getting us pregnant.

Ich Grolle Nicht.

ONE OR MORE OF THE ABOVE

What is love?
Is it someone you can't live without?
No
That's called obsession
Is it someone that your eye adores?
No
That lacks discretion
Is it someone who makes you feel alive
When life made you dead inside?
Is it one or more of the above?
I have no idea what is love

ARTIFICIAL LIGHT

SHE AWOKE AT TWO in the morning and could not fall back to sleep. It had become a habit now, her new routine. She averaged three hours a night, sometimes less, and it had been going on for weeks. From the time she awoke until the time the thoughts in her head lost their grip on any dreamlike sense of the world and her place in it, there was a fraction of a second in which she could exist without the knowledge she possessed those three hours before. This brief amnesia was the only respite she would have in a life she no longer recognized. She would close her eyes and remain still, listening for sounds—the rush of a passing taxicab, car doors opening and slamming shut—anything to distract her from herself.

The wedding was in three months and she did not love him. When it had been four months away she had not loved him, or five months, or six. Yes, six. She had realized it six months ago and could no longer deny it. Each month that she could not bring herself to tell him was another month closer to the wedding. To tell him was to hurt him, but to not tell him was to hurt him more, to hurt him forever. She couldn't bring herself to do it because she loved him. She loved him as a person—his manner, his habits—and she found out too late that what she loved most about him was the way he loved her. She had fallen in love with the way he loved her. It was a malleable love that she could hammer into any form, and she had molded it into a shape that looked exactly like the love she had always wanted. She could have continued to live with the fabrication had she not met someone who stirred something real in her. She had tried to forget this new person, but could not.

She lay in bed all day. Late in the afternoon she rose and put on her slippers and walked into the living room. She stood in front of the large window that faced north, out toward the Hancock Building and beyond. Somewhere in the enormous city below a taxicab drove her fiancé to her from O'Hare. It was dusk and the sun smeared red and orange light over the skyscrapers. It shown in her eyes. He would arrive soon. She imagined the scenario that played out each time he had visited in the past. He would be so happy to see her that he would hug her around the waist and pick her up in his arms and hold her against him. He would cup her face in his hands and kiss her cheeks, her lips; he would let her long hair slip through his fingers. After not seeing her for a month, his passion would be great. He would want to take her by the hand and lead her to bed, and she would let him, and she would die inside.

She had told no one else, not her mother, not her best friend. Instead she made herself say it to her own reflection in the mirror so she could hear it out loud and in her own voice. She would scream it and then sit on the edge of the tub and cry.

The rays of the sun grew faint and were replaced by lights in the buildings. The familiar patterns greeted her like stars—fixed, artificial flames to replace the ones she could no longer see. She wished upon one. There was one light in the Hancock Building that she saw night after night. She recognized it because it was one of the few that was visible during her insomniac wanderings around her apartment. Within that room was a person who also couldn't sleep. She wondered who that person was. She created a backstory for her that she embellished each night until it reached the level of myth. The person was a woman. She was happy and needed no one else. Her happiness was self-contained, did not rely on a man. She was sophisticated and uncompromising, sure of herself. This woman went through life without a single doubt. When she made a decision, it was final.

She wanted to be this other woman so badly. She wanted to be anywhere but here, waiting for the buzzer that would announce her fiancé's arrival.

The time came. She buzzed him. She waited.

In that short time, she saw things more clearly than she was ever able to see them. It was so obvious, so simple. A child could have seen it. She saw her life as the fantasy it was. She felt it die inside her, felt it end, and there was nothing she could do to save it. She saw their relationship spread out, not in years, but in miles. The distance had masked everything. Seeing him once a month had the effect of viewing art with missing lines, and her mind had filled them in and made it whole with connections that weren't really there. She imagined it all, and now her imagination had abandoned her.

She heard him at the door. She unlocked it and let

him in. He was so happy to see her. He picked her up, he kissed her. He told her how much he had missed her, that she was his whole life. Her tears fell to his shocked expression. What was wrong? he asked. She laughed at the simplicity of the question.

They laid together on the bed. She squeezed him tight and cried into his chest. What is it? She was so lonely, she said. He had no idea how lonely she was. He told her everything would be OK once they were together. The problem was that they weren't together. He started to talk about the honeymoon. She told him to stop. Didn't she care where they went? She said she did not. He didn't understand. He asked why. He wanted her to be honest with him. She said she was tired. He reminded her how many hours he had flown to see her. He said he knew what would take her mind off things. He kissed her, but she stopped him. What was wrong? he asked again. She stood up and paced along the bed in front of him. She looked out the window of her bedroom, but couldn't see her light. He told her to stop walking and talk to him. He said he wanted to know what was wrong.

She didn't love him. She said it to him finally because he made her. She averted her eyes as she said it in a voice that held the emotionality of a toaster announcing the morning bread. He asked "why" over and over again until the words lost all meaning and collapsed into discordant tones. From there they were cancelled entirely, when she could no longer hear him and could only watch the mute movement of his lips form the pucker of the "W" before widening into the contortion that completed the word, the one that conveyed their history together from first kiss to last futile plea, a mouth she had kissed so many times, but now never again. Why? She told him she didn't know.

Is there someone else? he asked. No, there was no one else. Is there someone else? Yes, she replied.

He rose and walked to the bedroom door. Maybe we should postpone the wedding, she said. He turned back toward her. No. This is all quite understandable, he said. This is all normal. Just pre-wedding jitters. She needed to come home. She needed to come to where he was, to live with him again. She needed to quit her job and leave this place. That would fix things.

He left the room and soon after she heard the front door open and shut behind him. She dried her eyes and walked into the living room and turned on a light. She looked out the window. She saw it. She saw her light shining high above the city. It was there as it had been all these nights. She wished she could trade places. She wondered if there was someone in that lighted room who looked across the sweeping landscape of the city at the light on in hers and wished for the same thing. She wondered if there was anyone there at all.

VOCABULARY

I kissed your mouth
for the last time,
though it came to me
as a surprise.
I thought there'd be
one more time
at least
to feel your mouth
against mine own
and move your tongue
with the instrument
of my vocabulary.
But the life ran out
for us, my dear,
and it seems as though
I missed the end,
and sit in the dark
watching credits
roll past
counting geese
counting couples
in the park
in the darkest black
the night can fetch,

Lures

as when the lights first
go out
and I am rendered
blind.
Until I realize
I am surrounded by stars,
so brilliant against
the ink smear
of night,
like when I stare
at paper white
and blank,
and all the promise
and horrors it implies.
I see the stars shine
in the eyes of another,
who looks somewhat like you,
the way you used to look at me,
the way I looked
reflected off of you.
I wonder what she'd do
if I told her so,
and told her that I wonder
how it feels
to kiss her cheek
and wait breathless
for an invitation
to her mouth,
to her tongue,

Artificial Light

the instrument
of her vocabulary.

THE PERILS OF BELIEVING IN SANTA CLAUS

HE SAT ALONE IN the dark and stared at the multicolored lights strung around the artificial tree. His wife had done all of the decorating again. He hadn't helped at all this year, unlike last year when he had at least hung the wreaths outside. With each passing season he had done less and less, leading up to the present display of guilt-free disinterest. Had there been any guilt left, it would have broken the inertia that fastened him to the sofa, to the cushion farthest from the kitchen and closest to the front door. The front door had changed. He noticed it back in April. It was the same unfinished, glossy color, still made of mahogany. He had measured its dimensions to make sure they were the same. They were. It wasn't something intrinsic to the door itself, he decided, but in its function, in the way it worked within its surroundings and what it represented: safety, security. The door had always been something that kept things out. Now he saw a new function, one he didn't like.

It bothered him that he felt no guilt. In the past he had felt it, but that was before he had quantified the way guilt ebbs with time. It does so at a constant rate, and there was nothing he could do to change it, nothing to hasten it along or slow its steady progress. All he had to do was wait, pour himself the glass of Maker's that rounded off the corners of each uninspired day, and squint. When he squinted, he no longer saw the tree. The garlands were gone, as were the old photographs, the heirloom ornaments, the novelty items she had hung with painstaking care. He couldn't see any of it. All he saw were the lights. They could have been the Manhattan skyline, or the strip in Vegas, or Bourbon Street, two days before Mardi Gras. They could have been any of those things, but they weren't.

He could almost hear the ice on the front steps harden as the temperature dropped. The ice in his glass had long since melted, leaving a thin layer of brownish water floating above the whiskey. He swirled the glass to mix it in, and took the last swallow before rising and walking into the kitchen where more bourbon awaited him in the back of the corner cabinet, the one near the microwave.

She sat in the kitchen, addressing Christmas cards at the table made for them by the Amish. She heard him approach and looked up at him through the glasses she had bought the previous month. She needed glasses now. He would too, it was only a matter of a few years. He went with her to pick them out, and wanted her to get larger lenses surrounded by black rims, something to make her eyes stand out and look even bigger. She didn't. She was strong-willed when it came to her appearance; it was one of the things he said he liked about her back when they first met. He liked her big eyes then too. They weren't big, but enormous; enormous and mint green. After he met her he told his best friend that he was "haunted" by them, and then endured his ridicule for the rest of the dinner. But over the years her eyes no longer had that effect on him. They seemed smaller to him. They also looked paler, washed out like an old photograph. He really didn't like her new glasses.

"Timmy asleep?" he asked. He reached far into the corner cabinet, not caring if she saw him, but practicing stealth out of habit.

"Yes, he went right out," she replied. "He's so cute in his new PJs."

"Yeah," he said absently.

She took out another return address label and fixed it to the upper left corner of an envelope. "I was thinking it'd be nice to take him downtown tomorrow," she said. "Santa is at Macy's."

"Tomorrow?" he said, and not in a way to promote the idea. He accompanied his question with the sound of ice cubes hitting the bottom of the glass. She looked up when she heard them. The freezer door shut and magnets hit the tiled floor; green plastic pine needles lay scattered across the kitchen threshold, near the refrigerator, clinging to the tile grout. "I have stuff to do tomorrow," he said. He bent down and picked up one of the needles. The floor was like ice.

"Tomorrow is the only Saturday left before Christmas," she reminded him. "I would have taken him earlier, but you said you wanted to go."

"I know, I know," he said. He stepped on the trash can pedal to open the lid, and let the needle fall, watching it disappear between the spaces of the other trash. "I do, it's

47

just that I have a bunch of work stuff, you know."

"A couple of hours out won't kill you. Who knows how much longer he'll believe in Santa Claus. This could be the last year."

"You said that last year."

"It could be."

"You said it the year before that too."

"I think it's sweet that he still believes."

"'Sweet' isn't the word I'd use," he said. He twisted off the cap and filled the short glass an inch below the rim. "I've been thinking about this," he said. He left the bottle on the counter. "He's nine years-old. Don't you think it's a little, I don't know, don't you think he should've figured it out by now? I was six or seven when I figured it out."

"Each child's different."

"Clearly," he said. "I hoped he'd be a little more observant, a little more…" He drank down a mouthful of the chilled liquor.

"A little more what?" she asked.

"Intelligent."

The word hung in the silence that followed. He was sorry he had said it. She arched her brow and straightened her posture. "You're questioning his intelligence?"

He was sorry he had said it, but not enough to back down. "That's not where I meant to go, but I guess I am," he said.

"That makes me question yours."

"Be serious."

"I am."

"I'm not the one who still believes some obese, elderly man delivers presents to seven billion people in one night." He smiled at his own joke.

"It's not about intelligence. It's about faith. One has nothing to do with the other."

"I never bought into that," he said. "When I was seven, not only didn't I believe in Santa Claus, but I knew where babies came from. I knew how they were made and everything—none of that stork business either, I knew the real deal."

"Congratulations."

"What I'm saying is I was curious. I wanted to know things, I wanted to understand why things happen. He doesn't seem curious at all. He just accepts things, whatever's told to him. Where is his intellectual curiosity? Don't you care about that?"

"I like that he's still innocent. There's plenty of time for him to know the truth about life."

"You got that right," he said, and took another drink. "But what if he still believes in Santa Claus when he's thirty-five? What then? Would you like that kind of innocence? No, you'd think there was something wrong with him, and you'd be right. There would have to be something wrong with him."

"Nine is far from thirty-five."

"It wouldn't be sweet, is what I'm saying."

"It could be," she said. Her eyes glistened.

"Yeah, but—

He started to say something, then let it die. He brought the glass to his lips again. He looked at her over the rim, watched her sign Christmas cards without asking him to help. She never asked him to help. She never asked him to do anything, never demanded that he do anything of any kind. Maybe that was part of the problem, that she had set the bar too low. Maybe that's why he had gotten so lazy. His friends all said he was lucky because he seemed to do as he pleased. He could go out as often as he wanted, not that he did, but he could.

That part of his life changed during the past year, almost by accident. He'd been staying later and later at the office, and then going out to bars with some of the young people right out of college or business school. Next to them he felt ancient. He viewed them as a different species. They had their own language, their own customs. They had their own look as well, especially the women who dressed in outfits better suited for a club than the office with lace tops and skirts that clung to their hips before flaring out and drawing the eye abruptly to skinny legs in black stockings. Their eyes popped from halos of poker-straight hair and smoky eyelids lined with black.

He made a mistake once. He had lingered too long, well after the happy hour people from work had dwindled to just him and a flirtatious young woman with large brown eyes behind black-framed glasses. She was much too young for him, or so he thought. She asked if he'd mind walking her home. She lived nearby and there had been an assault in the area. She couldn't be too careful. He walked with her down dimly lighted streets; he squinted at the lights and made them shine brighter. He swore to himself that he wouldn't go up to her apartment. They arrived at her door and she asked him up. He didn't want to be rude. When he left hours later, he swore that would be the only time.

Guilt ebbs with time at a constant rate. The measurement of it is something for an analytical mind. He watched her stick another return address label on an envelope. How could she not know? He was glad she didn't know, but it still bothered him. Where was her intellectual curiosity? How could she not know?

The silence caused her to look up at him. She smiled.

He spoke: "So why don't you still believe in Santa Claus?"

"How do you know I don't?" she said.

"So you do?"

"Yes, and I'm...how old am I now?"

"You're thirty-nine, darling."

"You're sweet, dearest, but we both know I'm forty-two. I've been forty-two for almost a whole year. That means soon I'll be forty-three."

"Funny how numbers work," he said. "We're all helpless captives of them, aren't we?"

"If you want to be negative, you could say something like that."

What's wrong with being negative, he thought. There's a name for people who are happy all the time. They're called fools. Having an analytical mind and seeing the world as it is can cause negativity, but it's better than being blindly faithful. It's better than believing in Santa Claus at the age of thirty-five.

"So you believe in Santa Claus even though you're

51

the one buying all the gifts?" he asked.

"Maybe I am Santa Claus," she said.

He laughed. It could've been the joke, or the booze, or a combination. "OK, Santa," he said. "What do I get?"

"Were you good this year?"

"You tell me."

She stared back at him. "You already know you're getting a new iPhone. But I don't think we should share an ID anymore. I read that if two people share an Apple ID like we do, they can sometimes get each other's text messages."

In one millionth of a second, her big eyes flashed at his, and the amount of information they conveyed surpassed what could be transferred and processed by all of the supercomputers in the world. She knew. She knew everything, and he now found it impossible that he ever thought she couldn't know. He could see now how much smarter she was, how much smarter she had always been. There was never any hope, never a chance she wouldn't know.

He put the glass down on the counter to silence the faint, high-pitched rattling of the ice. He stared at the glass until he could no longer avert his eyes. He looked at her.

"Do you know how smart our son is?" she asked, rising from the table. "His friend Jim was over the other day, and I heard Timmy confide that he doesn't believe in Santa Claus anymore, but that he plays along for our sake, because he knows how much it means to us. He's only nine. To have that kind of empathy at nine is remarkable, don't you think?"

She gathered the stack of cards. They were the typical store-bought kind, the ones with clichés splashed across the fronts in big letters. But inside were her personal notes, each one unique, meaningful and sincere. She signed them from herself, her son, and her husband, with love.

He watched her leave the room, and listened as the living room carpet swallowed the sounds of her footsteps. She turned and ascended the stairs and out of view. Still watching, he reached for the bottle but knocked it over. It hit the counter and spun a half turn, but he had nothing to clean up because it was empty.

MOLECULES AND MEMES

Molecules
and
memes,
We are caught here
In between them.
Getting crushed into broth,
or sown into the cloth
that keeps unraveling
before us.
Are you here to have a child?
Or to think of something strange?
Maybe both
Maybe neither
We are wisps
In the ether
Floating, diffuse
Of no particular use
To thought or to gene
When I don't even seem
to know why
I can't sleep

STAN SLADE AND THE CASE OF THE KILLER MEME

IT WAS THE WORST idea in the history of worst ideas. That's what they had called it. It was meant as an insult, but to Stan it was the highest form of praise. Bad ideas were the stickiest kind, the ones with an M-R5 rating on the Dawkin's Scale. He could still hear the voice of his first memetics teacher, Professor Nitsche, echo through the vast emptiness of the Blackmore Auditorium.

"The human mind remembers the best and worst of things," he'd say between shameful glances at the eager young girls scribbling away in the front row. "It remembers the edges of the bell curve."

If there was any truth to what Nitsche had taught him, then everyone in the world would remember the day Stan Slade came to Philadelphia. What lay inside Stan's head was an idea so revolutionary it would push the Declaration of Independence and the American Revolution to footnote status in Philadelphia's history. Stan came in search of a meme-gene crossover, something postulated by only the most fearless memetic researchers but something that had never been observed. The brightest minds in the fields of genetics, memetics, and human physiology said that a meme-gene crossover was impossible. Proposing otherwise risked all credibility—it was tantamount to publicly requesting a halt to funding or to publication in even the most irrelevant journals. But as is often the case with things deemed scientifically impossible, they become possible with the utterance of the word.

Stan raised his head against the shadow cast by the brim of his hat revealing weathered eyes that had seen too much, eyes that had looked outward and then inward and couldn't decide from which to turn. They scanned the darkening skyline of the city and fixed on the two sharp peaks of the Liberty Towers. Stan hunched his shoulders against a cold gust of April wind before he snapped the broad lapel of his rain coat up around his neck. He lowered the brim of his hat once more, pausing a second to enjoy the feel of the black felt between his fingertips. A storm was coming. He hoped it wouldn't ruin his experiment.

He stopped short of the concrete steps that led down to the Broad Street subway line, fearing the music of the subway buskers—the guitarists with missing strings, the trumpet players that were a hair too flat, singers who could not remember all the words. They were the worst: the singers. They made up words to a well-known melody, mutating even a pleasant meme into something that could take days to dispel. A chill passed through him as he remembered an incident in Chinatown a decade before. This required caution.

He descended, taking care to avoid the fresh wads of chewing gum in favor of ancient tar stains. Halfway down the steps he shot a quick glance over his shoulder. He couldn't be too careful. Earlier in the day he had picked up a tenacious meme that required something from the Beatles genus to root out. The meme was innocuous, a flippantly created melody with no intentional malice; even so, with his job description he could not allow himself to host such a replicator. He had profiled it in a matter of seconds: it was a standard one-four-five musical replicator, a bastardization of a popular rock and roll song from the previous century, employed to sell hybrid cars in this one.

But even this harmless jingle held danger, and therefore justified Stan's work as a detective in the memetic regulatory industry. A vague smile raised his upper lip as he appreciated the simplistic beauty of the process. The jingle sounded like so many others. It was able to confuse his brain, mixing with similar tunes so, before long, he would be humming something slightly different, which would then be overheard by another person, whose brain would do the same thing. His ability to understand how a rogue meme could turn a human brain into a breeding ground provided no immunity, and he gave the jingle its due respect, a respect he knew could not be returned. Memes were created and propagated by humans, but they were lifeless, given the illusion of life by the human mind and its penchant for imitation. Stan cycled through "Obla-Di, Obla-Da" off of the White Album. This was one rogue jingle that had met the end of the line.

But this other meme, the one he sought: that was something altogether different. They said a meme-gene crossover was impossible, but what did they know, and who were they to say so? And why had he rhymed that last thought?

He shook a cigarette from his pack of Red Apple

and stopped in the middle of the subway platform. In front of him a bum dressed in a schizophrenic patchwork of burlap sacks sewn together with coarsely woven string ranted incomprehensibly. Waves of commuters swept past him through billows of steam that rose from the subway tracks. White clouds converged on the burlap man, circling him like ghosts inspecting the tattered rag on his head and the cardboard boxes that served as his shoes. Stan squinted as he tried to make out the advertising on the boxes. He wondered why steam rose from a subway track.

He struck a match and cupped his hands to shield it from the wind of a distant train. The crackle of paper as he put the match to the tip of the cigarette was itself so pleasurable that he wondered if he even needed to inhale. He denied himself for a few seconds, teasing his addiction before the glorious first drag. He emptied his lungs and filled them again and watched the exhaled smoke mix with the tumult of steam. He studied the glassy-eyed faces of lawyers and commodities brokers and financial analysts as they passed, laptop-toting men with ears hard-wired to invisible devices buried in their suit jackets as their heads bobbed to the arrhythmic shuffle of leather-soled shoes on painted concrete. Where were the women? Why had he rhymed that earlier thought? Why were there so many businessmen on the subway mid-day? Why was he asking so many questions?

He refocused his mind on the McCartney tune. No, it was a Beatles tune, but it was written by McCartney. He remembered the arguments that echoed down the halls of the Dawkins Institute as they finally took to the monumental task of categorizing all memes. Did Obla-Di belong to the McCartney species under the Beatles genus, or the other way around? It became confusing very easily.

"Pardon me. Can you stake a fellow American a meal?"

The bum's question shook him from his analysis with its jarring and anachronistic level of diction. It was a voice belonging to a nineteenth century tale that did not fit the Depression Era content, Moby Dick meets The Maltese Falcon. No, not that film, he thought, and then churned through the taxonomy he himself had helped create: Visual Kingdom, Film Phylum, Talkie Class, Black and White Order, Drama Family, Action Genus, Western Species. Treasure of the Sierra Madre. But it could also be categorized as a burlesque, a parody of Sierra Madre used in a Warner Brothers cartoon in which Humphrey Bogart asks Bugs Bunny: "Can you help a fellow American who's down on his luck?" Same sentiment, same cultural context, different words: a mutation. If he didn't think carefully about it, Stan would be unable to remember which was from the original film and which was from the cartoon. And he didn't think either was from the book that was the original source of the meme. There's a name for that scenario, a name Stan himself had coined: a Burlesque Meme Mutation.   Ironically, the term never caught on, utterly failing as a replicator.

Stan looked at the bum once more and met his eyes. The bum smiled.

"How you doin'?"

Where had he heard that before? He chuckled to

himself. Where hadn't he heard that? He heard it often in this town: it was a colloquialism as catchy as a strain of swine flu. Not, "Hi, how are you?" Not, "Good day to you, Sir." But "How you doin'?" The bum asked again.

Stan marveled at the inner workings of the human brain, of how the man could effortlessly flip from a psychotic rant to an almost pedantic level of articulation, and then drop down to a studied provinciality with expert ease. It was a testament to the brain's complexity and a reminder that humanity had only scratched the surface of understanding it. Sometimes he thought there was no understanding of it at all.

Down the track a young Asian girl butchered Mozart on a cheap violin, but Stan appreciated her playing because it was the perfect background to the spectacle dressed in rags before him. He handed the bum fifty cents and then walked over to the girl and dropped a dollar into her bucket. She had earned more than his pity, despite her stained and faded dress and thousand-yard stare. It mattered to him that she had tried to earn it, especially in the city that launched the greatest meritocracy the world has ever known, the place where the U.S. Constitution was born, a document he admired as one of the deadliest killer memes ever conceived. To adhere to it is to shut your mind to any other philosophy of governance. Powerful, he thought, but nothing compared to the grand-daddy of all killer memes: the Ten Commandments. First commandment: Thou shalt not have other gods before me. With that one statement it slaughters every other collection of God-related memes. One had to stand in awe before it and marvel at the authors who possessed such a deep understanding of meme replication, and how to prevent it, thousands of years before such a thing was ever given a name.

Stan now searched for a different kind of killer meme, a literal one, one that could bring about bodily death through genetic change without the time required for evolution. He was removed from his position at the Dawkins Institute when he first suggested it. He still felt the sting of the great injustice, of the last presentation he was ever allowed to give in the Blackmore Auditorium, the one the board of trustees did not allow him to finish. Even old Professor Nitsche, his mentor and steadfast defender, stood with body and voice shaky from Parkinson's Disease and declared Stan's theory baseless and without merit, citing an appalling lack of evidence and adding that such a suggestion was too outlandish for even the most carelessly rendered science fiction.

This was Stan's chance to prove his theory correct and return triumphantly from the outer fringes of memetic research to where he rightly belonged: back at the Dawkins Institute, as its head. This is what had brought him to the City of Brotherly Love in the first place, but love was not what he was after. He sought hostility, and he knew where to find it: at the sports complex at Broad and Pattison.

He turned back toward the violin player as the incoming train blew past her, burying her well-intentioned musical transgressions beneath the howl of steel wheels coming to a stop against the rail. She continued to pull her bow across the strings, oblivious until the final pneumatic blast gave the coda to her performance.

"Keep practicing," Stan muttered with a tip of his hat.

On the train almost every seat was taken by Philadelphia Phillies fans on their way to Citizens Bank Park for the home opener. Auspicious, thought Stan.

A surge of riders pushed him further into the car and up against a pole. A sign above the doors informed Stan that he too could develop skills to pursue opportunities in electronics, web development, computer programming, criminal justice, or other of today's fastest growing career fields. He turned and looked down the length of the car.

Between an eight-year-old Main Line girl with the word "Juicy" embroidered on the seat of her sweat pants and an octogenarian shaking a filthy thermos at her with disconcerting glee, he could see a young woman in a light gray skirt suit and dark-rimmed glasses. Head down, she read from a yellow legal pad. She slashed the paper with her pen, flipped to a blank page, and began to write. Once he saw her, Stan could look at nothing else.

She was long and slender, and appeared so naturally at rest in the seat that Stan imagined she had been designed into it by Frank Lloyd Wright himself. Her lips were more full than thin, and turned up at the corners, giving her mouth the appearance of a subtle grin. She needed no lipstick or rouge, but wore them anyway. Her eyes were almost too far apart, and perhaps would have seemed so if not for their large size which, combined with the high arch of her brow, gave them a depth that contrasted the freshness of her face. Her skirt made no apology for her legs and the effect they had on men. Stan found it difficult not to stare.

As more baseball fans packed the train, they pushed Stan closer to her until he was grasping the metal bar directly over her head. He could see her reflection in the blackness of the adjacent glass. A Daily News lay in the empty seat next to her, opened to the sports section.

"Need a place to sit?"

The voice was soft yet assertive, and she did not look up from her writing when she spoke. She had noticed him notice her. Detective amateur hour, he thought, but then felt better about it. A woman like this would expect men to stare.

"Thanks, but I'm fine where I am," he replied.

She removed her glasses in such a deliberate way that Stan half-expected her to say that she knew about the affair, or knew where the diamonds were, or knew where he had hidden the gun after burying the body. She looked up at him with eyes that matched the color of her suit, only brighter and paler, made paler still by the jet black bangs and bob cut that framed them.

"This is all copyrighted," she said with a playful tap of her pen against the paper. "Just in case you get any ideas."

"You a writer?" asked Stan, with such a contrived aloofness that made him wince.

"Sometimes," she said, and then returned to writing.

A prerecorded voice soon announced that the train was about to pull into the Lombard-South Street station.

She did not move. Stan hoped her plans and his were the same.

"Headed to the ballgame?" he asked, but not wanting to sound too hopeful added, "You don't look like you are."

"Neither do you," she replied without looking up.

With those words Stan had the overwhelming sense that he had played out this scene before, that he had been on this train in Philadelphia as an alluring sometimes-writer scribbled down notes, read them, crossed them out, and then scribbled them again. He was certain he had met her before, but was equally sure he would have remembered. He would not have forgotten that face and those legs had they been on two different women; to see them together on the same woman made him hear wind chimes and smell honeysuckle.

He inhaled deeply through his nose, but then a thought occurred to him, a dreadful thought: perhaps this wasn't a chance encounter; perhaps the familiarity she invoked was not misplaced, not an artifact of insomnia or loneliness or paranoia or a synergistic monstrosity of all three. Perhaps she had been sent by his enemies—those at the Institute who wished to discredit him. He could not forget what he learned in the Los Feliz district of Los Angeles: that sometimes murder could smell like honeysuckle. The detective in Stan awoke from the brief spell the bespectacled stranger had cast upon him.

"What are you writing about?" he asked.

"I write short stories," she said. "At least I try."

She uncrossed her legs and then crossed them

again—an act that should not have seemed as intimate as it did to Stan.

"Sometimes I ride the subway on my lunch break to watch people," she continued. "I take notes, sketch them out, look for inspiration."

"And have you found any inspiration?" He sounded too eager.

"Well, I hadn't," she replied, then stared up at him again. "Until just now."

Stan could see the barbed hook protrude through his upper lip and felt her tug on the line.

"So what do you write?" he asked, feeling shortness of breath. "Melodramatic-harlequin-vampire-zombie-coming-of-age stories?"

She laughed. "No. I'm partial to comedies."

Stan chuckled through his nose, sounding snider than he had intended. She didn't seem to notice or care.

"I started out writing more serious topics, but not anymore," she said.

"Why not?"

She tucked her dyed hair behind her left ear. "People don't care about serious topics anymore. They just want to laugh. Or read about sex. Or both."

The train came to a dead stop twenty feet shy of the platform, causing all who stood to lurch forward and claw at the metal poles to keep balance. As the train started up again, Stan could hear rowdy laughter, muffled at first, but then gaining volume as the train pulled into the station and stopped. The subway doors opened and a small group of very loud men poured into the remaining space.

There were four of them, and each wore a white Phillies jersey with red pinstripes and the name of a Phillies player on the back. Each jersey looked two sizes too small, and the bulging musculature of their upper bodies tortured the fabric and seams of the obviously well-made shirts.

"No way, man! Maria Rosato?" said the man wearing the Utley jersey.

"Yes he did," added the man wearing the Moyer jersey.

"What can I say? I'm a sucker for big cans," said the man wearing the Victorino jersey.

"Oh, daddy, I hope you wrapped that shit good."

"And he should know," added the man in the Werth jersey.

"Don't worry. I wrapped it like a Christmas present, daddy."

"Just for her."

"Yeah, only I ran out of paper, know what I'm saying?"

The Victorino fan grabbed himself halfway down his thigh and gave a tug. Despite the close quarters he gesticulated wildly as he spoke, and with each rotation of his wrists the cuffs around his biceps seemed to cut off circulation, engorging the veins in his arms until they popped from the flush surface of his skin.

"Check it out." He reached down his shirt and pulled out a gold crucifix. "My cross was hittin' her forehead so hard, she went home lookin' like a vampire who lost a fight with a priest!"

A roar of admiration filled the subway car as Stan

watched the men gather together, arms over each other's shoulders, and mutate a Bernstein-Sondheim meme from West Side Story.

"Maria! He just banged a girl named Maria!"

Stan looked down at the girl, who wrote furiously onto her notepad between furtive glances at the new passengers.

Stan knew he had to act swiftly, but did not know why. He could not intellectualize his actions, but pushed past an elderly man and a pregnant woman and stood by the muscle-bound quartet to shield the girl from them. Her gray eyes looked up at Stan and the corners of her mouth rose more than slightly.

Stan closed his eyes and steadied his breathing. He hadn't touched liquor, but he felt drunk. He had acted without thinking, without purpose. He searched his motives to understand what had happened to him and why his heart pounded in his chest. He had lost perspective. He had lost distance from himself and his subject matter. He cycled through Obla-Di once more and remind himself why he was in Philadelphia. "I am here to conduct an experiment. I am here to conduct an experiment." He recited the mantra until it mixed with Obla-Di to ill effect and he had to stop. He kept his eyes closed, but could not shut them tight enough to block the quartet's singing. He kept his eyes closed, but he could still see the spark in the willing gray eyes of their next victim. Stan's thoughts became jumbled as he fought back feelings so wantonly destructive they could only be jealousy. He wanted to open his eyes but was afraid to catch a glimpse of his reflection, afraid to discover he had grown fangs and claws to match how he felt on the inside.

He heard Professor Nitsche's voice: "Take inventory of what you have, not of what you want."

It worked. He rediscovered what fate had given him: four prime subjects on which to test his hypothesis. He had failed to realize this because he had taken his eye off the goal, and he had done it for the worst possible reason. He did it for a dame; for a woman he didn't know and could not possibly care about; for a black-haired, gray-eyed, comedy-writing twist.

Stan opened his eyes. He turned to her and she stared back at him with such genuine concern in her big, probing eyes that he nearly succumbed again.

"So where's Joey?" asked the guy in the Victorino shirt.

"Ah, he's depressed again."

"Depressed? What could that human hump possibly be depressed about? He lives at home with his mom and doesn't even pay rent."

"Yeah, and he's got us."

"I miss that fat bastard."

The gray-eyed girl rose as the train pulled into the station at Snyder. She squeezed past the elderly man and pregnant woman; unlike Stan, she politely excused herself first. Stan's pulse rate quickened as she approached. Her head was down, but she looked up at Stan when she reached him. She stood only an inch or two shorter than his six feet.

"Excuse me," she said as she squeezed between him and a college student who was texting on his phone. Her left breast imperceptibly brushed against Stan's chest.

"So what are we going to do with Joey's ticket?" one of the four asked.

Her gray eyes turned back toward Stan, and she gestured toward them with a nod. Somehow she knew Stan did not have a ticket to the game.

Her presence among the four men brought about an abrupt silence, but they did not act as Stan thought they would. They did not smirk, they did not make catcalls, they barely looked at each other and made no other visible form of communication.

"Excuse me," she said as she walked past them to stand in front of the door. Stan could see her looking at the Victorino fan's reflection in the subway-door windows.

The train stopped and she exited without looking back. As soon as the doors shut, they started.

"My God, what I would do to that!"

"Sweet Mary, mother of Jesus!"

"Madone!"

"That looks like a lot of fun right there."

"You should've asked her if she wanted to go to the game. Christ, do I have to think of everything?"

The girl had liked these men, or at least found them interesting. Stan wondered if she even knew why herself. What Stan found interesting was the recursive nature of memes, how they are both products of and driving forces behind cultural change. The four men were a good example. Somewhere in its history, Philadelphia became less Philadelphia Story and more Rocky, less playground of the elite and more home to the underdog—visceral, dirty, tough, dangerous, passionate, filled with working-class romanticism, savage and tender. Formal recognition of this metamorphosis came when the Rocky statue was placed in front of the Philadelphia Museum of Art: as grand and discordant a mixing of memes as Stan had ever seen.

The train pulled into the Pattison station. The doors opened and the baseball fans flooded the platform and drained into the large escalators that led up to the street. Stan hung close to the four as they boarded the escalator.

"Too bad we're not playing the Mets today," said one. "Remember when I puked on those assholes wearing the Mets gear?"

"Classic."

"Yeah, you don't come to our house wearing a fucking Mets hat."

"Hey," said the Utley fan. "We gotta unload this ticket, daddy."

"Why don't we just keep it? Whoever we sell it to will be sitting with us. What if we don't like him?"

"Well, just don't sell it to a jerk-off."

"If I didn't want to sit with a jerk-off, I wouldn't have invited you."

All but the Utley fan laughed.

"Pardon me, fellas," said Stan. "I'm looking to buy a ticket."

The four men fell silent and looked down the escalator toward him, suspicion in their eyes.

"What's that, buddy?"

"I'll buy your extra ticket," said Stan.

They looked him up and down. "You don't look

like you're heading to a ballgame. You look like, uh, like an I-don't-know-what."

"Well, I am going to the ballgame and I need a ticket."

"You gotta be kidding me."

Stan took out his pack of cigarettes and packed them against the palm of his hand. "I overheard you talking about how you need to sell one, so I thought I'd ask." Stan pulled out a cigarette and let it hang loosely between his lips; it flopped up and down as he spoke. "But if you'd rather not, it's no skin off of my nose. I'll find another one somewhere else." Stan lit up his cigarette and took a long drag.

"Hey, you're not supposed to smoke in here," said Utley.

"What are you, the cigarette police?" Stan said casually. "Don't tell me a tough guy like you is gonna whine like a twist about a little cigarette smoke?"

"Like a what?"

His friend laughed. "A twist. You know, a woman. I heard that shit on some old movie."

Veins bulged in his neck and biceps around the Utley shirt. "You calling me a woman?"

"Not at all," said Stan calmly. "With the kind of hardware you have strapped to those arms, you look like you could break me over your knee. For that you would have my respect, but just know that you'd take some losses of your own. But you may not want to take such a threatening position. It's poor salesmanship."

The Victorino fan laughed. "I like this guy."

"What's up with the raincoat and the hat?" asked the guy in the Moyer shirt.

"Forecast called for rain," said Stan.

"Yeah, it did," added the guy in the Werth shirt. "I heard that on the news."

"Look fellas," said Stan. "You have a ticket to sell, I'm looking to buy. If you make up your minds before we reach the top of this escalator, we can do business. If not, there will be many other people outside trying to sell tickets." He took a long drag but didn't exhale all at once, instead letting the smoke escape with his speech. "And to show my appreciation of your hospitality, I'll buy the first round once we're in the ballpark."

"The ticket was twenty-eight bucks."

Stan reached into his wallet and pulled out two twenties.

"I don't have any change."

"That's all right," said Stan. "Keep it."

The group of five left the station and walked out into brilliant sunlight. A cool wind blew the remaining clouds into New Jersey while echoes of the Phillies PA announcer pulled the Broad Street Line commuters toward the stadium. Stan walked past truant college students and businessmen alike, all high on cheap beer and lighter fluid from charcoal grills. He walked past barefoot girls dangling their smooth, seventeen year-old legs over tailgates of F150s as men threw a football around the parking lot. Off in the distance, the retching of an inexperienced drunk accentuated the melancholy of a Springsteen song playing on a car radio.

Citizens Bank Park loomed over them, but Stan didn't see a state-of-the-art baseball arena. He saw a massive laboratory where ground-breaking memetic research was about to happen, a historic scientific event that would be unknown to any of the forty-thousand-plus Phillies fans there to watch Cole Hamels face the Washington Nationals. Stan could feel the electricity in the air flow through him and raise the hair on his arms. He looked at the faces of those who had come for entertainment. How could they suspect they'd bear witness to an experiment equal to Galileo dropping balls from the Leaning Tower of Pisa. He ran up ahead and bought two hats from a street vendor.

They passed through the turnstiles into the park, and Stan went to find beer. He knew how important it was to gain the trust of the subjects when conducting an experiment, to keep their confidences and honor any promises given. Stan ordered light beers from one of the concession stands on the two hundred level. He handed one out to each of the guys.

"Thanks for the donkey piss, daddy."

The seats were in section four hundred thirty-four, a section somewhat removed from the action on the field but very close to where the real action takes place in Citizens Bank Park. Philadelphia fans had long been known for their inhospitable treatment of other teams' fans, the Phillies players themselves, and each other, and most of the newsworthy examples of this behavior occurred in the higher levels. But it wasn't until a week-long battle with meningitis that the reason for this came to Stan.

Feverish and exhausted but with a heightened

perception, he had actually seen the virus inside his mind as it spliced with a thought. He hypothesized that it was the proximity of the virus to his brain that made the meme-gene crossover possible. It was all conjecture, but the pieces seemed to fit. He studied the events that led to his illness and the role each could have played: that a virus had caused the meningitis while he was working eighty-hour weeks on a difficult case that had filled his mind with negative memes and anger. Stan had been very, very angry that day because that was the day he had found out about the decision of the Dawkins Institute board. He believed that great anger was the key, the spark that ignited the crossover.

Stan settled into his seat and removed his fedora. It was time for part one of the experiment. He pulled the Phillies cap he had bought outside the ballpark snuggly over his head. He attempted to observe the effect of a physical representation of the Philly Fan meme on himself. He closed his eyes. He drank his beer. He waited.

The first pitch was a four-seam fastball for a called strike.

"Yeah, Hamels!"

"That's it!"

"My man!"

The second pitch was a curveball that missed the outside corner of the plate.

"What the fuck was that?"

"Send him to Reading!"

"Your mother!"

Stan felt no change in himself, no onset of a genetic change that could offer a reason for the heightened levels of adrenalin and testosterone of those who came to this ballpark.

Hamels retired the side, but not before Cristian Guzman doubled to left field.

"I'm slittin' my throat over here!" yelled one of Stan's seatmates.

The game was scoreless at the top of the second inning, and all four of Stan's friends were on their third beers. Hamels missed with a fastball and a cutter to Josh Willingham, but his next pitch found the strike zone along with the sweet spot of Willingham's bat. Willingham took the pitch deep to left field as all stood to watch Ibanez sprint hopelessly to the wall. The ball sailed over it for a homerun. The stadium, as a living, breathing entity, groaned.

"You suck, Hamels!"

"I hope your kids get run over by a gas truck!"

"I don't think he has kids, daddy."

"Then his sperm. I hope his sperm gets run over by a gas truck!"

Stan, who had not observed anything close to the results he hoped to see, decided it was time for part two of his experiment. In his preparations, Stan considered the possibility that it was not anger which triggered the crossover event, but fear. That was why he had bought the second hat.

The skies were clear and sunny over Citizens Bank Park. Winds blew in from the west at fifteen miles per hour. The Victorino fan had just raised his hand to hail the beer man—"Yo, daddy! Beer! Yo! How 'bout some beer!"—when a full sixteen ounce cup of beer hit him on the back of the neck, drenching his shirt and covering the people in the row in front of him.

"What the fuck?"

"Go back to Jersey, you prick!" yelled a voice from above.

He turned to look back at the upper rows, but stopped dead when he saw Stan was seated with his shoulders hunched and his hands folded between his knees, and a Mets cap on his head.

The fans above hurled more beers at the men.

"You motherless prick!" He shouted at Stan.

"I told you he was a jerk-off!"

"Get that son of a bitch!"

They lunged at Stan, but their advance was squelched by a deluge of beer and plastic cups. "Goddamnit! Come here, you bastard! I'm gonna puke on you!"

The guy in the Utley shirt grabbed Stan by the front of his coat, pinned him down with one arm, and then put his finger down his own throat to force himself to vomit.

"Hold—" Utley retched. "Hold still, goddamit—"

Stan did not wait for him to complete the task. He broke free of his grasp and half-ran, half-fell down the rest of the rows toward the exit.

"Grab him!"

Stan dropped the Mets cap on an empty seat, and it was picked up by an elderly man who looked up to see a guy in an Utley jersey projectile vomit two inning's worth of beer and ballpark franks all over his face and chest.

Stan ran until he reached the subway station, and

threw money—more than he owed—into the window slot. He ran down the long escalator and thrust his arm through the closing subway doors, squeezing through them just as the train pulled away.

The train rolled out of the station, and Stan sat breathless. He had not observed anything resembling a meme-gene crossover at Citizens Bank Park. All he'd observed was the result of decades of memetic conditioning: Philly fans were supposed to act that way, so they did. As he tried to recall the day's events, he felt the memories of them slip away, disappearing like pages torn from a yellow notepad. The only thing he could remember was the woman on the train.

The train lumbered into the Snyder station and stopped in its usual abrupt manner. The doors sprung opened and he saw the long legs he could never forget. She sat on a metal bench and wrote onto her notepad, but looked up the moment he looked at her. She rose and pushed her way through the people leaving the train, reaching it just before the doors closed.

She stood next to Stan in front of the doors. The train started to move. He smiled at her.

"How'd the writing go?" he asked.

"Could've gone better," she replied. "I couldn't focus."

"How so?"

She shook her head. "I wanted to write this hard-boiled detective piece, and then I tried to lighten it up with some comedy. But it got a little weird at the Phillies game." She held up her Daily News sports section with an article about the previous day's home opener.

"Weird's not bad," he said.

"No. It isn't," she said. "I wanted to capture what it's like here, the scope of it all, but my head became filled with too many things." She tore the pages out of her notepad and crumpled them into a ball.

"I'm sorry," said Stan.

"No. Don't be," she said. "It's not your fault. I like the way I wrote you, but I'm not sure about the ending." She looked at herself in the subway door window. "Surprise twist endings are so M. Night Shyamalan."

"Yes," said Stan as he reached into his coat pocket for his cigarettes. "But they're irresistible."

She nodded. "That meme is a killer."

She chuckled. It was time to get back to her office. She had taken too long for lunch as usual, and she would have to walk as fast as her short legs could carry her. She hoped that the preppy subway guitarist at the Market Street station was gone. He had played Obla-Di, Obla-Da incessantly, as if it were the only song he knew. That was a very sticky song, a very sticky meme. She knew she would be humming it to herself for the rest of the day. It was too bad the other guitarist wasn't there, the grungy one with the sadness in his voice. He usually played a lot of Springsteen.

GARGOYLES

Walk to the edge
where gargoyles keep
mute vigil
A step
then no going back
No matter
for we
are invisible to them

SING FOR THE LONELY

SHE WATCHED THE SMOKE cloud hang above the heads of the skinny women and then disperse as the front door let in a blast of autumn air. The smoke diffused into the hair that hung down her back, baby-fine wisps that matched the smoke in both form and caprice, with a color that matched the gray walnut planks jutting from the low ceiling of the bar. The smoke embedded itself between the fibers of her oversized clothes and penetrated the wood of the tabletop in front of her, the one on which her six beer cans rested and waited, moistened by the dew that rolled down their sides and trapped the smoke for a later release in her apartment. She would take the six-pack out of the bag and set it down onto the coffee table where it would warm and dry until it freed the smoke from the aluminum walls and made her living room smell like the bar. She wouldn't feel so alone.

She came to the bar only on karaoke night, although she never sang. She always sat by herself, but she liked it because she could hear and watch people. On this particular night she held a newly purchased vinyl record. Vinyl albums were the only things she collected, and she collected them because she loved them. She loved the groves in the vinyl that vibrated the needle in infinite frequencies and produced sound as if by magic.

She liked the building and its history, a pub constructed in 1873 that stood alone on a hill overlooking her small town of Coopersville. The hillside was famous for the gusts of wind that swirled around the edifice, sometimes blowing fifty miles per hour. The building would give and sway as the stresses drew moans from the dead wood.

She had finally figured things out that day. Wind is a force of nature, and nature traps things. The water traps the smoke. The can traps the water. The vinyl traps the sounds produced by those long dead. God trapped her in a body no man wanted to touch. He hid a passionate mind behind a face no one would love. People had been cruel to her, but no one could hurt now because she had her books and her poetry to protect her.

She learned the truth at seventeen, that her real name was Tess and that she was made to pull the Durbeyfield plow through a field stained red. She learned the truth at eighteen that the only roses she would ever have were ones she stole from Grierson Flowers after evading the proprietor's watchful eye and the proprietor's husband who never said too much.

When she was twelve she awoke covered in blood. It was a Tuesday in May. She didn't scream because she was expecting it. She was finally a woman and her mom bought her flowers. Ten years later she learned the truth at twenty-two, that although she bled as other girls did, for her it held no purpose.

She prayed to God the way she was taught.

"Why, dear Lord, is there no one who loves me?"

The Lord's response was stretched out over many years and bore many forms, for the Lord is everywhere.

"My precious, precious child," said the Lord. "You are ugly. I cannot allow you to reproduce because your offspring will be ugly and make my creation ugly."

"But I have things others don't," she said. "Why are they worth less?"

There was no response.

"My voice is beautiful," she said.

"Yes," said the Lord, although she did not hear him.

On the night she had decided to sing, the announcement of her song nearly broke her resolve. She rose and made herself small. She found the spaces that existed between the others, the skinny women who made themselves skinnier with a smile and a furtive roll of the eyes, the men who stood firm, oblivious to all but the flow of their own self-aggrandizement.

The cadence of the opening drums matched her slow approach to the microphone stand. She kept her eyes down as she plodded ahead; the floorboards announced her weight with a creak on each step. She took the microphone as Roy Orbison's "Crying" poured from the speakers, the same song on the vinyl record she clutched against her breast. When she came to stand in the spotlight, the crowd turned away, not wanting to see the embarrassing spectacle. Then she closed her eyes and began to sing. At once the crowd became a collection of individuals who turned to her as if shaken from a trance. One by one they left the shelter of their drinks and banal conversations as she told them her true love was gone. She made each person in the crowd feel the full measure of her loneliness and of their own, the kind they all tried to ignore by surrounding themselves with other people and other things. Her beloved was gone, and she wanted everyone to know that she would never know happiness again, that the world was now a meaningless place where she would always be crying. The real tragedy is that her lover was gone because he had never existed. The melancholy captured in her voice made everyone feel it, the false urgency of loss. She whispered it confidentially before unleashing the latent intensity of the song's despair.

The Coopersville wind pushed against the building as if to topple it and deliver it in pieces to the town below. As the air that carried her voice met the wind, there was resonance, and together they altered the structure. The boards twisted imperceptibly, the ancient nails raised from the surface of the wood by unmeasurable amounts.

"Crying" rang out the way human beings really cry, unrestrained and without pride, the wail of those who have never known the pain of losing someone because they never had someone to lose. The voice shook the graying walnut planks with its penetrating sadness and longing for a best guess, for something real in lieu of approximations of real emotion she only felt in her dreams. She stood before them as nature's forgotten, one who had been discarded before she was born—the lonely who would be left crying always.

The song ended and she left the microphone stand and walked through the crowd. It parted before her with the silence of a confessional. Everyone in the crowd was alone, and they immediately ordered drinks to help them forget it.

Outside, the wind blew the smoke from her clothes and her hair. She held her six-pack and vinyl record as carefully as priests carry the chalice and communion hosts. It was a beautiful night, a starry, starry night. It was a long, long time till morning, but there were no fires to build up high, only a warm bath and the shiny, silvery release that lay on the sink waiting for her.

No one saw her again, but soon after her performance a myth grew from the collective imagination that the building was haunted. On some nights, particularly during a storm or when the wind blew so powerfully against the building that it deformed its structure, patrons reported hearing a woman singing. They heard her with such clarity, more than anything else in their digital world. They heard the fear in her voice and the way it receded as she sang Roy Orbison's bittersweet song. Long after any genes she might have passed onto children would have been diluted out of existence, the sounds of her voice remained embedded in the structure of the building and made it sing for the lonely.

ZOLOFT

I thought I was bipolar
Like the Old Man and the Sea
But the doctor didn't share
My suspicion
As she clicked her Zoloft pen
And wrote on her Zoloft pad
And looked at her Zoloft poster
And drank from her Zoloft mug
Guess what she prescribed?
Guess the way I died?
With a rope bought at Walmart
With the prescription change

DAD IN THE MACHINE

DAD WAS LAID TO rest on a Friday. I know it was a Friday because it rained, and I remember thinking how I always get depressed when it rains on Fridays, and that it was just as well it was a Friday funeral since I would've been depressed anyway. The service was beautiful even though the flower arrangements outnumbered the mourners and the priest kept mispronouncing our last name. The cantor sang "Here I am Lord" with such genuine emotion that it nearly punctured the blanket of numbness covering the whole of my body. Dad's brother, Uncle Rob, gave the eulogy because no one else volunteered, and he did a decent enough job considering the two of them hadn't spoken in over a decade.

I stood in the second pew looking stupidly at the casket. I didn't want to, but it was right in front of me and I would have had to make even more of an effort not to look at it, which would have only made me dwell more on how my father had been drained and embalmed and bolted into the coffin where he'd remain for eternity. My brother Tommy stood next to me, emotionless—more so than I—and silent and still, but with an air of something resembling humility, which is unusual for Tommy no matter what the occasion.

It was just when I had taken to wishing that

someone would slap me across the face so I could feel something—anything—that I lowered my head to pray and caught sight of Tommy's hands as they grasped the back of the pew in front of him. They looked just like Dad's hands when he was young, as they appear in a mental image of a description of a memory I might have had as a child, of a solitary figure seated in a recliner with his hands resting on the arms of it, and me, standing next to him, invisible, as his eyes remained fixed on the glowing images of more interesting people doing more interesting things in the electrified box in front of him. I'd watch him until the unruly hairs from my pigtails made accidental contact with his hand, causing him to jerk it away. Those images are all that remain, and that's when it hit me that he was dead. I would never again see the creases in his face which gave it such distinction, or inhale the smell of his clothes as I folded them and put them away. The last time I spoke to him was the last time I'd ever speak to him and I felt him fading away more quickly than I thought possible. The only proof he had ever existed were the genes making up half of who Tommy and I had become.

I looked at Tommy and he mouthed something to me which only became clear later. He mouthed the words "He's not there."

I didn't cry in the church. I didn't cry when I got home or when my neighbor told me how sorry she was, or when I looked through the mail addressed to Dad and wondered how long before even his name would disappear from records. I never cried, partly because I knew Dad would not have cried for me. Dad was never one to express emotion, and I had long ago decided it was because he had no emotions to express. I tried not to be angry or resentful about it because I knew it wasn't his fault. It was the way God had made him. He was an iceberg of a man, a man who did not cry at his own father's funeral, just as I did not cry at his.

But I did feel something soon after. It did not hurt or make me feel sad, or even weary or anxious, at least not initially. It was something I couldn't comprehend at the time and have no hope of understanding even now. It began on a Saturday, two weeks after the funeral, when Dad was delivered to my door.

He came in a very plain cardboard box, the kind Amazon uses to deliver books. But there were no labels or postage, and it didn't arrive bearing any insignia of UPS or USPS or FedEx. He lay there on my front porch, waiting for me to trip over him with my morning coffee.

I never got the chance. Tommy pushed past me, knocking me against the already deformed screen door and spilling my morning coffee all over my feet. It was piping hot.

"Hey!" I yelled.

Tommy said nothing.

"What is that?" I asked.

He snatched the package off the porch and shot me a look as if I had inconvenienced him somehow. He stormed back into the house and let the screen door slam behind him.

I called after him.

"Tommy! Tommy, what is that?"

93

It was the last I saw of him that day.

Over the week that followed, Tommy's behavior grew more and more strange. Tommy is eccentric and a bit of a recluse anyway, but he stopped going to work altogether after the package arrived and spent every waking hour in the basement, which was odd even by his standards. Tommy is a computer whiz—it's what he does for a living—and he is so secretive about his work that I jokingly tell people he works for the CIA. He would only emerge from the cellar when he had to get more supplies, and he'd return from his missions with arms loaded with cables and connectors and things that looked like props from a science fiction movie set.

For my part, I spent the nights of that week going through Dad's few remaining possessions, and I was amazed by how few there were. Dad read voluminously, but would only read books borrowed from the library. He played several musical instruments, but didn't own any. He had no car, very few pictures, and his entire wardrobe could fit in one small suitcase. He was a minimalist to the extreme, and it occurred to me that he had always been prepared to vanish without a trace, without warning, and without saying goodbye. In the end, that's exactly what he did.

Among the handful of pictures he left behind was one of him and Mom on their wedding day. Dad, tall and plain, and Mom, short and strikingly beautiful, they stood before the photographer while Mom smiled and Dad looked off to the left with a blank expression that almost evokes pity. I often wondered what he was looking at or what he was thinking about when the pictured was taken. A hint of the answer revealed itself to me years later, within my own face in my own wedding picture from my own failed marriage.

Two weeks after the package arrived—on a Sunday, four weeks after the funeral—Tommy's behavior turned from strange to bizarre. I realize that people deal with grief in different ways, that some throw themselves into their work or a new project, as Tommy was doing, while others, like me, use the time to reflect. I gave Tommy his space and I tried to respect our different ways of mourning even though I couldn't imagine what he was doing in the basement at all hours of the day and night. I left him alone because I knew that's what he wanted. I also hated going into our basement and did so only to do laundry. Our basement was not a very welcoming place. It was downright creepy, with stone walls that molted decaying whitewash, and low-hanging radiator pipes that made the six feet of height between the dirt floor and the petrified joists seem lower. I'm taller than Tommy, so I had to walk around hunched over to not smack my head against the iron pipes or invite dust-laden cobwebs to infest my hair. There was a large piece of asbestos that kept me away from the boiler, one that Tommy was too afraid to remove himself and too cheap to hire someone else to remove. Still, none of this was creepy enough for Dad, who told the eight year-old versions of me and Tommy that the ghost of a 1940s gangster named Mr. Spinalzo lived in the basement and would "rub us out" if he ever caught us down there. That kept us out for a good long while, which is what Dad wanted. It's what the adult version of Tommy wanted of me.

I opened the door to the basement.

"Tommy?"

There was no answer.

"Supper's ready."

The only sounds were of him tinkering with his electrical supplies. He was no doubt seated at the workbench Dad had built from two-by-fours and the old laminate kitchen countertop.

I stepped onto the landing, which creaked horribly as my foot came down upon it. The sound was a composite of all the other footsteps that had ever fallen there. The sounds became embedded in the wooden boards over years and years of pressure and deformation, and somewhere within them the sounds of my father's footsteps had been stored, ready to be released. I took another step and heard them come out, like putting a needle down on a vinyl record. Dad was there in the stairwell with me, his presence as real as Tommy's a few feet away.

I reached for the old radiator pipe repurposed as our stair railing and walked down the steps, slowly, one foot at a time, not stepping down to another until both of my feet came to rest on the same one. The stairs were open in the back, and even as a grown woman I held my breath as I descended, waiting for Mr. Spinalzo to grab my ankles and pull me into the darkness forever. That's when I heard it.

Tommy, do you think you could get me a job where you work?

There was no doubt it was Dad's voice. That was one of his favorite things to say to Tommy. To the untrained ear, it sounded nice, a father asking his son to get him a job so they can work side by side, but Tommy and I knew differently. The the intention behind it was hurtful. It spoke of Dad's view that what Tommy did for a living was so easy anyone could do it. Someone with no skills and no training could walk in from the street and work side by side with him. It was also Dad's reminder that Tommy did not have a management position and couldn't hire him if he had wanted. Tommy and Dad never got along.

Tommy, you're supposed to be smart?

I heard Dad's voice again and realized that Tommy must be playing the tapes of Dad we had found in a cardboard box in the attic. He searched like crazy for them months before Dad died. I thought nothing of it, only that his time would have been better spent talking to Dad while he was alive rather than preparing to listen to tapes of him when he was dead. I tried not to judge, but I did judge him, secretly, to myself.

"Listening to tapes?" I asked. I was at the foot of the stairs with the largest radiator pipe inches from my forehead. Tommy was seated at his workbench with a small black device, about the size of a laptop. He turned his head slightly, with the least amount of effort or acknowledgement, and smirked at me in his superior way.

"They're not tapes," he said.

97

"They're not?"

"No."

"Oh." I recognized the start to one of our typical conversations. "What is that?" I asked, pointing at the device.

"It's Dad," he said nonchalantly.

"Oh." I paused. "What do you mean?"

"I'm speaking English, Kell."

"I know what the words mean," I said. "I just don't understand what you mean when you say 'It's Dad'"

"I don't know how else to say it," he said.

"Well think of a different way to say it." I tried to keep my voice even.

"OK." He cleared his throat for effect. "This isn't a tape. This is Dad's brain." He put his eyelids at half-mast. "Is that better?"

This explanation made even less sense. "What do you mean by that?" I asked.

He looked at me, exasperated.

"Don't worry about it," he said finally. "You're not good with computers, Kell."

It's amazing how someone who's known you your whole life can cut you down with one short sentence. When Tommy said, "You're not good at computers" he was referring to a very painful experience I had involving social media, a humiliating one that cost me a job I loved teaching an introductory class to drama and playwriting.

"Dinner's on the table," I said as sweetly as I could.

He turned away from me and went back to the

device. "I'm not hungry." He dismissed me with a wave of his hand, and I turned and hurried up the stairs. The creaks and groans of the staircase filled my head with images of Dad walking up and down it endlessly, descending night after night into his dark shelter guarded with ghost stories and neglect, retreating to it for no other reason than to escape from his children. I walked into the kitchen and stared at the meal I had prepared, at the two place settings I had set instead of three. It was like there had always been only two place settings. Normally I would have wrapped Tommy's dinner and put it in the refrigerator for him to eat later, but that night I threw it in the trash. I ate alone, and went to bed early without even clearing the table.

Three nights went by before Tommy joined me for dinner again. Chicken is one of the few things Tommy likes to eat, so I prepared a whole one cooked all day in a crockpot with white and sweet potatoes, carrots, celery, onion, rosemary, and thyme. I prepared a salad of romaine lettuce—mainly for myself—with grape tomatoes, fresh carrot slices, cucumber, and an olive oil balsamic dressing. Buttered mini-rolls cooled in a wicker basket covered with paper towels.

We sat at our large oak table that Uncle Rob had made. The two leaves I put in it the year before were still there because I enjoyed the distance from Tommy that they provided. We ate in silence for most of the meal, until I asked him where the sounds of Dad's voice had come from.

"They came from the device that came in the mail."

"I guessed that much," I said. "What is that device?"

"It's Dad's brain." He said it as casually as if he were commenting on the dinner rolls.

"I don't know what you mean when you say that."

"It's not a past recording, or it is, but not in the way you'd understand. It is not something that was recorded exterior to Dad's brain, like with a tape recorder, or digital files saved to your phone. It is a recording like a saved memory, like a memory you recall from your own brain, where the sounds and images are retrieved and put into the cognitive part, the part where you exist and where you can make sense of it."

"I'm sorry, Tommy," I said, "but I don't understand what you're saying."

He didn't get upset like he did before. Instead he tried in earnest to explain it to me. Looking back, I think he wanted someone to tell, someone who understood. "The device in the basement contains Dad's brain," he said. "Not the organic part, but all his memories. His entire brain was mapped and downloaded to magnetic media."

I focused on a practical question to keep him talking, since I didn't understand anything else. "When did this happen?"

"Within five minutes of his death." He spread more butter on his already buttered roll and stuffed the whole thing in his mouth. As he chewed, he spread butter on another roll, a big heap of butter that melted immediately and ran down the sides. "Do you remember right after he died," he said, talking through the mashed buttered bread in his mouth, "Do you remember how I ushered you to the cafeteria to get a cup of coffee?" He did do that. I had to think about it a little, but he did.

"That's when they came and took his body," he said. I could see the bread stuck between his teeth as he spoke.

"Who came?" I asked. My heart started to beat quickly.

"People from Synapse."

"What's Synapse?"

"That's the company that provides this service."

"Why do you always have to joke around?" I said. "Dad isn't cold in his grave, and you're making jokes."

"Dad's not in his grave. He's downstairs on my workbench."

"It's inappropriate."

"It's better than being in a grave."

"Stop it!" I shouted. Tommy did not flinch.

"You don't believe me?"

"No."

"Really?"

"How can I?"

"Have I ever lied to you?"

"Lots of times."

"Have I ever lied to you about something important?"

I didn't know, and I didn't want to try to think of a time. I ignored him and dished myself out some more carrots.

"What would it take?" he asked.

"What?"

"What would it take to prove to you that it's Dad down there?"

I didn't know. I wanted this joke to end. But I didn't want to give him the satisfaction of getting to me. He thinks he's so smart, and it was the way he sat here looking at me with that smarmy look on his face which forced me to continue the conversation even though I wanted it to end. I continued it, knowing it was exactly what he wanted, and ironically proving to myself that he was much smarter than me just like I thought.

"Tell me how you heard about this service," I said.

He slumped in his chair and lowered his head to glare at me from under his Jack Nicholson eyebrows and shaved scalp. He leaned forward into the table and stood, leaning across the table toward me, farther than his five foot six inches of height seemed to allow, and extended his chin over the bowl of white potatoes that no longer produced steam.

"Are you serious?" he asked. "That's what you want to know? I just told you that I downloaded our father's brain onto a disk, and you want to know who in the marketing department at Synapse did an extra good job of targeting my specific demographic?"

I guess it was a stupid question.

"People in-the-know know who Synapse is," he said. "Let's leave it at that." God, he can be infuriating.

"What happened to Dad's body after they took it?" I blurted out. "Did they map his brain in the hospital room, or did Igor take it into the janitor's closet?"

His face relaxed. "They took his body to their

mobile lab parked outside the hospital, removed his brain, and delivered his body to the mortician."

"Just like that?"

"Just like that. Synapse is a model of efficiency. It also helped that Dad wanted a closed casket."

That perked up my ears. "No," I said. "That's not true. You are the one who wanted a closed casket. Dad never said anything about it, and I certainly wouldn't have chosen it."

It took something as simple as catching him in a trivial lie which made me start to think he was telling the truth. I decided to play along, to see what other lies would come out, what other twisted logic could trip him up and reveal his true motive. I tried a different approach, one that would appeal to his passion.

"The technology to do this doesn't exist," I said with an authority I didn't have. Tommy jumped on it.

"The technology has been around for years, but it's far from ready for wide commercial sale. It lies in the bleeding-edge technologist niche market. When a mature technology hits the market, the R&D behind it is decades old. Microwave ovens were invented in the 1950s, thirty years before they became commercially available and found their way into domestic kitchens where even housewives could figure out how to use them."

Tommy had little respect for women who worked inside the home, and that went doubly for our mother.

I sat with my mouth open, recapturing some of the magic of my high school performance as Helena in *A Midsummer's Night Dream*.

"Tommy, how could you do something like this without asking me?" I acted hurt.

He smiled broadly. "Because I knew you'd never allow it. Because you lack vision, because you'd be unable to see the gold mine we have in front of us."

As expected, he didn't miss an opportunity to point out his superior intellect. To him, I was and will always be a hometown girl, hopelessly provincial even though I went away to college while he stayed here. Tommy has never left my parents' house. I returned only to take care of Dad after he became ill.

"What gold mine?" I asked.

"We have complete access to Dad's memories. We can run queries, find information." This new line of questioning had knocked Tommy out of the doldrums. He was getting excited. "And not just his memories. We can have some real fun and run scenarios, to see how Dad would react. And someday soon," he said, attacking another buttered roll with the table manners of a dog, "the programmers at Synapse are going to come out with a way to animate him."

His words rose the flesh on my arms. "Animate him?"

"Yeah. It'll be like Dad has come back from the dead."

Had Tommy said, "Come back to life," I don't think I would have been as horrified. "Come back from the dead" sounded monstrous, even though it's used several times in the gospel. Jesus raised Lazarus from the dead, he didn't "bring him back to life." Somehow, the thought of what Jesus would or would not have done did not make me feel any better.

I tried as best I could to hide my anxiety by asking more questions. "Yeah, but what kind of life would that be for him?" I asked. "Is he even alive in there? Is that him, or just his memories? If it is him, will he know what's going on?" Thoughts flooded my mind chaotically; I couldn't piece them together into an intelligent line of questioning.

"I don't know," said Tommy, unperturbed, "but I'm sure the Synapse folks will figure it out. They think of everything."

We ate in silence for a bit longer, until Tommy looked at me. I half-smiled at him and he looked back with squinted eyes and a brain behind them that crunched through scenarios from a lifetime spent observing my behavior.

"Kell," he said. "I know you don't believe a word I've said, but I will prove it to you. In the coming weeks, I will dig up something that only you and Dad knew—some experience only you and he shared—and you will be unable to doubt me, and you will treat whatever I say going forward as the gospel truth."

That got to me, it really did, whether I believed in what he said or not. *Turn of the Screw* can still make my blood run cold even though I don't believe in ghosts, and by the time I went to bed that night, the one undeniable truth was that, real or not, Tommy had conjured the ghost of our father and it hung heavily under our roof.

I wouldn't wish the next few weeks of my life on even the people who fired me from my teaching job. I had found myself in a Shakespearean tragedy, with ghosts that roamed freely and a family member who spent every waking hour plotting my demise. I felt trapped in my own house, and even on the rare occasions when I ventured outside, my mind was still there, wondering what Tommy was doing in the basement, worrying that he was "running queries," whatever that meant, and trying to dig up information about me and Dad.

I already had my fill of people digging up information about me without my consent. I found no humor in the irony that Tommy had alluded to my firing from school while he was trying to dig up private information he could use to hurt me. In the same way, what happened to me at school should never have happened. I had posted pictures of myself drinking beer and wine while on vacation. I wasn't doing anything wrong or illegal, but when I returned, the school board fired me for inappropriate behavior. The novelty of such a privacy invasion was already wearing off, and not much attention was paid to it by the news media, not that I wanted attention. That experience changed me. For all the years I had been carelessly posting my personal information and pictures online, it never occurred to me what I was really doing. I was giving the world an inaccurate self-portrait, the most narrow view into myself possible. The things I posted did not represent all of who I was, but that's all I shared with people, so that's all they thought of me. I am more than the sketch I created online, and the companies that mine social media data know this too, and that is why they dig even deeper.

Tommy stopped coming to dinner. I watched the weight fall off of him from our accidental encounters in the kitchen, upstairs hallway, or passing in and out of the bathroom. He looked strung out, and I found myself worried about him even though he was making my life needlessly difficult. I had never seen him so focused on anything before, and was sure he wouldn't notice if our house was on fire.

One night I turned from the kitchen counter holding a bowl of peas and saw him sitting at the table. He looked so out of place that I screamed and dropped the bowl. Peas and ceramic shards went everywhere.

"I failed," he said. There was a look in his eyes of an unquiet mind.

"What?" I bent down to pick up the peas, but he told me to leave them.

"I didn't find your proof."

"You didn't?" A feeling of relief swept over me, a kind I hadn't felt since I was in high school and found out my mother didn't have breast cancer. There was nothing in that machine, this was all a joke, a way Tommy had chosen to deal with his grief—a very selfish, childish way, with no regard for my own loss.

He shook his head. "You win."

"I didn't know we were playing a game," I said.

"I couldn't find anything that I didn't already know about your relationship with Dad."

"No?" This was not over.

"I found all kinds of other stuff, though."

A knot formed in my stomach. "Like what?"

"Do you want to know what Dad really thought of Mom?"

My heart thumped around disjointedly in my chest as he spoke. This was not over by far. Whatever Tommy had been trying to accomplish, he was still striving for it. Part of me stood in awe of him, wondering where he had learned to be so cruel.

"Do you want to know if he loved her?" he asked.

"No."

"I always wondered about that. Didn't you?"

"Please stop."

"I have the answer now."

"Tommy, this isn't funny."

"I know you're curious. Do you want to know if he loved her?"

"This isn't real. What you're doing isn't real."

"If it isn't real, then what's the harm?"

"Why are you doing this to me?"

"Stop being a narcissist. This isn't about you."

There was no end to his absurdity. A narcissist doesn't take care of her father while her brother refuses to lift a finger to help. "I don't need an electronic device to tell me whether or not Dad loved Mom," I said. "Of course he didn't love her. He was incapable of loving anything."

"You're wrong." He rose from his chair and walked slowly toward me. "He did love her, at least he thought he did. I can only go by his memories, and we are the narrators of our own memories. It's a shame we're so unreliable."

"Tommy," I said. "I know you're going through something now, but I am too."

"It's funny how the power of technology can still surprise me."

"Tommy, I'm worried about you."

"Do you want to know what he thought of you, Kell? I mean, really thought of you?"

Ten years after my mother's breast cancer scare, new test results came back positive, and she was gone within six months.

I think I shook my head. I'm not sure.

"I searched and searched for something," he said, "some kind of shared experience that the two of you had, something only you two would know about. I even looked for memories of abuse, but there is nothing. It's like, I don't know, like he never had a daughter. I know that's a shitty thing to say, and it's not what anyone would want to hear, but that's what the data suggests. I'm sorry."

He looked sincere. He looked concerned about me for the very first time.

"You're making that up!" I screamed.

"No I'm not."

"Yes you are!"

"I'm not."

"Stop!" I tried to regain my composure. "It doesn't matter. I don't know if that thing downstairs is real, and if it is, I don't understand how it works and have to rely on you. That's the problem. It's like I'm illiterate and I'm listening to you read me the Bible, not knowing if what you're reading is really in the book or stuff you made up."

"For instance," he said ignoring me, "I was able to find the name of the priest who married them. Did you know his name? I didn't. I don't think Mom or Dad ever spoke of him. It's Father Lafferty. I later checked the church's records, and guess what I found? That was the priest's name. I also learned that Dad was concerned on his wedding day because he had dated the girl that Uncle Rob brought as his date. The girl was still hung up on Dad, and she just happened to be the woman Uncle Rob ended up marrying later that year, making the woman none other than our own Aunt Diane. She stood near them and stared at Dad while they were taking wedding photos. Dad was distracted, and it made him look off and out of the frame. Dad had been fooling around with Aunt Diane up until the wedding day." The room began to spin on me. "And do you know where Mom and Dad stayed on their honeymoon in Atlantic City? It was the Shelburne Hotel, room 106, but then they switched rooms because Mom didn't like the view. Their new room was number 213. I validated all of this with external sources."

I wanted to laugh at everything he said, at the insanity of it, but what Tommy had learned made perfect sense. The trivial details about their wedding meant nothing: it made sense because Dad always treated me as if I didn't exist, even while I provided his care before he died. Nothing could have proven Tommy's claim better than the discovery that I was nothing to my father. Tommy had his proof. He had convinced me more than if he had produced a written assertion of Dad's apathy that he himself had signed, more than if he had found the names of a million priests, and a million room numbers of a million hotels.

"You have no right!" I shouted. "You have no right to do this!"

"I have every right to do this!" he hissed. His voice dropped to something guttural, and his face contorted into a shape that matched. The anguish inside of him, the hurt that must have been building his whole life, made itself visible to me. I had never seen anything so grotesque. "The man gave me nothing while he was alive. He had no humanity, so I have no problem treating him like a machine now, because that's what he was."

"According to you, that's all any of us are. Would you do this to me, Tommy, after I die? Would you reduce me to a bunch of bytes on a hard drive?"

"You beat me to it," he said. "Why don't you put that on social media? You can quote me."

I took out my phone and threw it at his face as hard as I could. He ducked, and it shattered against the wall. I ran out the back door—not stopping to put on shoes—and kept running until my side and my feet started to hurt.

All around me, everything seemed to stop, as if I had run so fast that I had become the only dynamic part of a still-life world. I imagined everything digitized, the way it would be if my brain were on a disk, if there were no physical world, but everything instead existed as pixelated images that were created on the fly. That is what Tommy believed. He used to lecture me that the reality we think we live in isn't physical, but a virtual one, and always has been, and that's why the future can't be predicted because we all create it just before we move through it. As distasteful as the idea was, it comforted me when my parents died. It meant that they weren't dead since they, along with me, had never really been alive.

I walked up and down my neighborhood streets. I thought of the night the nurse had called to tell me that Mom was near the end and that I should get to the hospital quickly. I called to tell Tommy, but only reached his voice mail. He claims he didn't get the message until it was too late, but I don't believe him.

Mom had gone down to seventy pounds. Large bruises marked her arms where the chemotherapy had been injected. Her skin had lost its elasticity and resembled colored tissue paper. Her thick head of dark curls was gone, leaving sporadic strands that made her look unkempt.

When she opened her eyes and saw me sitting beside her, she lifted her head up with what looked like every bit of strength she had.

"Kelly." She looked at me with eyes filled with sympathy. "This is so hard." And then she died. I was the only one there.

For years I thought about what she said to me. At first I thought she meant that dying was what she found so hard. The longer I lived without her, and the more interaction I had with my father, the more I concluded that the thought of leaving us alone with Dad is what she found so difficult. Her last words were an apology for dying first.

Whenever Mom and Dad would fight—and by fight I mean Mom yelling at Dad who would sit in his chair watching TV like he didn't even hear her—I would always get in the middle, try to be the diplomat. Tommy would always run to his room, and I'd find him there in front of his computer, writing programs. As a boy, he created an imaginary cyber world where he had complete control over everything. I did it too, later in life, with the plays I'd write. On the page, I could control the characters' every word, the outcome of every conflict. My characters behaved exactly as I wanted them to behave—until I handed the script to actors. That is where Tommy and I differed. My characters could surprise me, sometimes in profound ways if I was lucky enough to get some good actors. But Tommy's programs were different. He had absolute control over how they functioned. Any surprises to Tommy were called defects.

Standing there, I wrote Tommy into an improvised play and staged it in my head. What was Tommy's motivation? What was his character arc in this story? I read it and rehearsed it over and over again in my mind. I tweaked it, and ran it again until it became obvious. I knew what Tommy was trying to do and why. I wanted to run to him and throw my arms around him. I wanted to tell him I understood and then take care of him like I hadn't been able to do while Dad was alive.

I arrived home and threw open the deformed screen door. I ran down the stairs to the basement, immune to the history of the stairs assaulting my senses. I stopped with both feet on the dirt floor and looked at Tommy hunched over the machine. Dad was there.

Tommy, I am so proud of you.

I ducked beneath the pipe and walked next to

Tommy, shuffling my feet so I wouldn't startle him.

Tommy, did I ever tell you how much I respect you?

I stood next to him. A book called "Synapse Hacks" lay beside him.

I love you, Tommy.

He turned to me. His face held the pained ambivalence of someone who has just completed a quest.

"Did you hear what he said? Did you hear that, Kell?"

I heard it. I had heard every word Dad said and even knew why he said it. Tommy made him say it.

Couldn't he see what he had done? Couldn't he see what I saw, that none of this was real, that all he did was force Dad to say these things?

Tommy stared at me with a bittersweet expression. I grabbed his hand and pulled it in close, caressing it. My hair fell down upon it, and he didn't pull it away. The tears rolled down my face and dripped onto my feet. They were piping hot.

My words came out mechanically. There was no thought, no reasoning to them. They came out as involuntarily as a laugh or a sob.

"Can you make him say those beautiful things to me?"

STRAY COLORS

Wavelengths
pulled from
crest to crest
shifting light
into the red
I can't see
but sense you there
Your stray colors
left a trail

LURE OF THE UNATTAINABLE

LILLY WENGER GREW UP on Copper's Island, a small fishing town off the coast of Massachusetts. She and her parents lived next door to another young couple with a daughter of the same age named Mary. Lilly and Mary became very close—closer than sisters—which in some families isn't hard to do, but since neither girl had any siblings of their own and often felt the loneliness particular to only children, each girl became the axis upon which the world of the other spun. Their families liked to say that when one girl took a breath, the other exhaled it for her.

The girls went to school together from kindergarten through high school graduation, and in every milestone of each other's lives they were steady fixtures, like the bedrock of the island itself, timeless and secure.

When the girls discovered boys, it did not change their relationship at all except to bring them closer together. They told each other everything about their latest crushes, and they never competed for the same boy since their tastes were very different. Lilly liked smart boys and Mary liked jocks.

By the time they reached their early twenties, both decided it was time to marry. Lilly had become engaged to Philip, who would become the island's only doctor, while

Mary fell in love with a popular high school athlete named Pete. No one was surprised when they chose the same year to marry, or when they conceived children within the same month. If anyone thought it was a remarkable coincidence that they gave birth to their sons on the very same day, they kept it to themselves.

It was in this way that Michael and Frederick, or Freddie as he was called, came into the world destined to be best friends, the brothers each would never have, since, like their mothers, they were to be only children. Their close friendship was something Lilly and Mary both wanted, and they did their best to make it a reality. They breastfed their children side by side; the first pictures taken of the boys were of them lying next to each other in Lilly's playpen. When the boys were older, the women sent them off on weekend trips with their fathers who taught them how to fish and set lobster traps. Mary and Lilly took them on ferry rides to New Bedford where they would walk among the colonial brick homes and enjoy the Seaport Cultural District. The boys played on the same three sports teams: baseball in the spring, football in the autumn, and basketball in the winter.

Every Sunday the two families dressed in their best clothes would walk to church to attend mass together. Michael and Freddie would sit and listen to the story of two brothers who were torn apart by jealousy and murder when one received more love and praise from God. They heard Jesus teach the importance of forgiveness to his apostles, many of whom were fisherman like Freddie's father. After mass, the six would eat brunch together and talk about small town things.

Lilly and Mary tried their best to create a mold for a unique and lasting friendship between the boys, into which they poured everything they thought would guarantee the desired cast. But in order to make it seem possible to themselves, the mothers had to ignore what anyone else around them could plainly see. Their boys were as different as there were ways to be different. They were different in appearance and deed. Michael had his father's intellect, introverted nature, and interest in math and science. Like his father Philip, Michael would rather spend a day reading than outside playing football. Freddie was very physical and athletic like his father, Pete. There were no bookshelves in Freddie's room because there were no books. Unlike Freddie, who never contracted so much as the common cold, Michael was a sickly child with a condition that caused fluid to build behind his ear drums and rupture them, resulting in infections that required surgeries. These surgeries prohibited Michael from submerging his head in water, and as a result he never learned how to swim, something that became a source of shame as a boy growing up surrounded by water.

Despite their differences, the two boys loved each other, and not simply as brothers would. They loved each other as friends who would have chosen to have each other in their lives.

During their early schooling, one boy would help in an area where the other boy was deficient. Michael helped Freddie with his classes and homework, and Freddie helped Michael become a better athlete and have more confidence.

While both improved a great deal, they never achieved as a high level of proficiency in the other's skill, but that was expected. They both knew their own talents and had no unreasonable expectations. As Freddie became the most sought after kick ball player at recess, Michael cheered him on. When Michael won the school chess championship in the fourth grade, Freddie bragged to other kids that Michael was his best friend. What neither would ever know was how much they longed for the other's talents. For all of Freddie's prolific athleticism, he wanted nothing more than to be thought of as smart, to get the best grades on the math and English exams like Michael did, and have the ability to write the stories in the library books he too often had difficulty even reading. Likewise, for all of Michael's academic prowess, he dreamed about hitting the home run to win the big game and being mobbed by his teammates the way he'd seen happen to Freddie. In sixth grade, when each child was asked to describe their hero, Michael and Freddie wrote about each other without the other ever knowing. There was balance in their lives since Michael was as good a scholar as Freddie was an athlete. They went on that way for years, supporting each other and thinking of each other as the person they wanted to be.

Nature would not let this continue indefinitely. The year the boys turned thirteen marked great changes within them. It made them see their female classmates in ways they hadn't before. The girls for their part, who underwent similar changes, discovered Freddie and Michael with new eyes as if they hadn't gone through grade school and middle school with them for eight years. It would have been sublime had they seen the boys as equally as the boys saw each other, but the ways of nature lack nobility and are riddled with inequality, unfairness, and brutal competition. All of the girls found themselves much more attracted to Freddie than Michael.

Despite Michael's intelligence, it took time for him to understand the new way of things. Once he recognized his own sexuality, there was an initial phase of denial, a time when he clung tenaciously to his childhood routines. Like most boys, he was slow to admit that he wanted the attention of girls, but it became undeniable as his adolescent desires invaded most of his waking thoughts.

With the start of the school dances, a familiar pattern emerged with Freddie holding court with the prettiest girls in their class and Michael hanging out with other shy boys on the perimeter of the gymnasium watching. Michael spent a lot of time watching.

In tenth grade, Michael watched a beautiful girl with honey-colored hair named Lynn play field hockey after school. Freddie introduced him to her and they became close friends. Michael decided he was in love with Lynn because of the pain he felt in his chest whenever he thought of her. He loved her sweetness and intelligence during their many conversations, and her ruthlessness on the field as she wielded her field hockey club with the ferocity of a savage. Michael watched one day in eleventh grade when she and Freddie started dating. He heard Freddie describe their sweaty fumblings in the back seat of his father's Pontiac and in his bait shop. Sitting next to his best friend in mass on Sunday, Michael heard the preacher say that he should not covet anything that belonged to his neighbor. It was then that Michael decided to go far away to college. He decided to become a physician and return to the island only to take over his father's practice. His plans took him to California.

Freddie proposed to Lynn shortly after graduation and convinced her to abandon her college plans by making it a choice him or college. She chose him. Freddie started working in his father's bait shop, offering a new twenty-four hour bait delivery service to night fishermen. Freddie was out most nights delivering bait and often left Lynn home alone. While making his deliveries, Freddie tried to picture where Michael was, what he was studying and if he was still the smartest kid in his classes. He wondered if Michael had found a new best friend.

Michael dedicated himself to his studies and only came back to Cooper's Island for two occasions: the death of his mother, and Freddie and Lynn's wedding for which he was the best man. He did not return to the island for good until he finished his residency.

His father, Philip, retired shortly after Michael returned. Philip was a widower who had grown quite lonely, and Michael found it natural to move back into his parents' home.

On the night he returned, Michael arrived on the ferry and saw Freddie and Lynn with their three children waiting to welcome him home. They hugged and kissed him. Michael said how big the children had grown, and how well everyone looked, and how the island hadn't change a bit, and other obligatory things. They drove Michael home and escorted him to the door. When Philip opened the door a cheer of "Surprise!" rang out as what looked like the entire population of the island stood in the foyer and hallway of his house. Michael looked around at the faces from his youth, a little more wrinkled, a little more gray, but as bright as he remembered them. He felt someone squeeze his hand. It was Lynn. "Welcome home," she said.

Freddie and Lynn insisted on having Michael and his father to dinner once a week, on Sundays like they used to do, for brunch, along with Freddie's parents. "Lynn takes the kids to mass, but I hardly go anymore," said Freddie when Michael asked him about church.

During those brunches, it seemed to Michael that Lynn was keenly interested to hear his opinions about things like world events and politics. Freddie and Mary often led games which kept the children occupied while Philip and Pete played Horde Chess on a mahogany board Pete had made thirty years earlier.

One Sunday, Freddie, Philip and the grandparents took the children to the park and left Lynn and Michael to clean up. Lynn mentioned how it was nice having another adult to talk to. "You know Freddie," she said, "he's a big kid." Michael asked her if she was happy, which he immediately regretted and apologized for asking.

Lynn was silent for a long time, until she replied, "There are good and bad things about marrying when you're young." Lynn handed a newly washed plate to Michael who dried it with a towel. "I look at you and all you've accomplished. I'm fascinated by your mind, Michael."

"I've always loved you," he said.

Lynn acted like he hadn't said anything, and changed the topic. Freddie returned with his children shortly after, and Michael went home to drink himself to sleep with a bottle of bourbon.

Michael skipped brunch for the next three weeks. After the third time, he received a phone call from Lynn on a Monday night. She said simply, "The kids are in bed. Freddie's delivering bait. Come over." With those words the affair between Freddie's wife and his best friend began.

Michael felt horribly guilty about the affair, but not enough to counter the elation he felt about being with Lynn. He felt as if he were correcting a cosmic mistake, one that had prevented he and Lynn from being together all along.

The following months were the happiest of Michael's life and the most confusing. He had always thought of himself as a good person, and here he was doing something so unquestionably wrong that he no longer knew what to think of himself. He wanted Lynn to leave Freddie, but he never asked her because there was something not quite right between them, something in the feel of her when they were alone together, the response he expected from her when he touched her that didn't ring true. The last time they were together, she broke down and told him she couldn't do it anymore. She still loved Freddie. She said that she had been lonely, and that while she cared for Michael a great deal, the affair had to end. She begged him to never tell Freddie what they did, which made Michael chuckle, as if telling Freddie was exactly what he had been planning to do.

Michael did not feel sad, not the way he thought he

would. He mostly felt relief. He had spent most of his life wondering if there was anything there between him and Lynn, and now he knew that whatever there had been between them, it wasn't what he had hoped. The best part was that he no longer had to sneak around and betray the trust of his best friend. He made up his mind to make it up to Freddie without him knowing. He would be the best best friend in history, the best friend Freddie deserved.

A year after the affair ended, Freddie invited Michael to do some night fishing. Freddie had taken the night off from his bait service and "wanted to enjoy fishing for a change." Michael did not like going out on boats—at night in particular—because he couldn't swim. But he remembered his oath of being there for Freddie, and he accepted the invitation.

Well after sundown, Freddie and Michael set out on Freddie's boat, headed toward Vineyard Sound. It was a beautiful night and the stars and moon shone brightly off the water. Michael and Freddie had hung out many times since the affair ended, and nothing seemed out of the ordinary. They had just finished casting their troll lines when Freddie turned to Michael and asked, "How could you?"

The meaning behind the words did not click for Michael who responded, "How could I what?"

"You know," said Freddie.

And suddenly Michael did. In an instant, the tranquil setting transformed into one brimming with malice. Still, Michael convinced himself that he did not know what Freddie meant, that he could not mean the affair.

"Can you be more clear?" Michael said.

"How could you fuck Lynn?" Freddie said. "Is that clear enough for you?"

Freddie stood in the boat and loomed large over Michael.

"Please sit down," Michael said. He felt his insides lurch forward as if the earth had stopped spinning. He looked around but could see nothing but the man standing in front of him, the man he had known all his life.

"I want you to explain yourself," said Freddie. His voice quivered despite how much he tried to keep it even.

"Sit down, Freddie."

"Tell me!"

"Just calm down and I'll explain. What did you hear?"

"Lynn told me everything. She was in hysterics, begging me to forgive her."

"She did?" This was the most devastating news Michael could hear. "Why would she do that?" he said, without meaning to say it out loud.

"Because she has a conscience, unlike you."

Michael looked Freddie in the eyes for the first time since the accusation. "It's not what you think."

"No?"

"I love her, Freddie. I've always loved her."

"So do I, Michael. That's why I married her."

"You don't understand. I thought we were meant to be together. That's why. But now I know. I know that we weren't. She's meant to be with you." Michael looked nervously at Freddie's feet on either side of the boat, the way the boat rocked with the shifting of his weight and let in small amounts of water from over the sides.

"Please sit down," Michael said with panic in his voice.

Freddie did not move right away, but eventually sat back down in his seat.

"I'm sorry, Freddie," said Michael. His own voice sounded strange to him, like another person, a very desperate person. "I don't know why I did it. I guess I've always loved her, ever since high school—

"My god, Michael, that was forever ago! You're talking about high school? This is about my family. This is about you and me."

"It's not forever ago to me," Michael said. He looked into the blackness beyond the boat. He could hear waves hit the port side with increasing power. "What were you going to do out here, Freddie?" he asked.

Freddie looked straight ahead, out onto the small waves breaking against the buoy. He didn't answer.

"You brought me out here all alone," said Michael. "It's night, it's in the middle of the Sound and you know I can't swim. You could easily overpower me. What were you going to do?"

Freddie didn't answer.

"Were you going to throw me overboard?"

Still Freddie said nothing.

"Were you going to drown me and make it look like an accident?"

Freddie shifted in his seat. "I don't know what I was going to do."

Michael looked up into the sky for the hope of seeing even the smallest bit of light. There was nothing.

"I wouldn't blame you," Michael said. "I deserve it. I deserve to be among the bottom dwellers."

"How could you do this to me, Mike?"

Freddie put his head in his hands and sobbed so violently that it shook the boat back and forth. He cried for a long time. He cried until all that existed was his crying. It affected the tides and dimmed the starlight. It gathered mass and gravity and pulled everything toward it, the waves, the shoreline. It pulled the water so taut that a grown man could walk on it. His tears spilled over into the water and raised sea levels around the globe.

Michael looked at what he had done, and he wanted to hide himself because he was so ashamed. He looked at Freddie and awoke as if from a deep sleep, from the hiatus he took from the morality of his parents, of his mother. It ended abruptly as he himself emptied a lifetime of latent envy and exposed regret out of his eyes.

"Stop crying," said Freddie. "I'm the only one who has the right." Freddie wiped his own eyes. "I wasn't going to kill you, Mike. Best case, I was thinking that maybe you'd feel so bad you'd jump overboard yourself."

Freddie looked at Michael's startled expression and let out a deep, genuine laugh. Then Michael laughed, nervously at first, but then like he had heard the world's greatest joke. Both men laughed so much their sides ached as the sounds of laughter echoed across the Sound. The laughter soon died.

Freddie looked at Michael. "You know," he said.

"I'm not very religious. I rarely go to mass anymore, but I've been thinking a lot about forgiveness and what it takes to forgive someone who did this horrible thing to me. Catching your best friend and your wife having an affair is every man's worst nightmare. You've made me live every man's worst nightmare, Mike."

Michael stared down at his feet as the boat continued to rock. He felt ill.

"I remember," said Freddie, "when we'd go to mass when we were kids and sit next to each other. We'd hear the preacher talk about Jesus and what he said about how we should forgive no matter what. But you never know how hard it is until you're called to do it."

Michael looked at him. "Do you forgive me, Freddie?"

Freddie was slow to answer, then sighed heavily.

"I've thought about this," he said, "and I've decided that I do forgive you, Mike."

"Really?"

"Yeah. I just wanted to make you sweat a little to see if you were sorry."

"I am," said Michael. "I really am."

The two men sat without speaking as the waves rocked the boat.

"I guess I should head back to shore," said Freddie.

"*We*, right?" said Michael. "*We* should head back to shore."

Freddie gave Michael an ambiguous grin and started the engine. The wind created by the boat blew against Michael's face, and suddenly the thought of reaching shore became the most horrible thing in the world. They hadn't gone far when he told Freddie to turn the engine off.

"What?" said Freddie.

"Turn it off."

"Why?"

"Please. Just do it."

Freddie turned off the engine and sat down across from Michael. "What, you want to do some night fishing now?"

"How will I know?" said Michael.

"How will you know what?"

"How will I know that you really forgive me?"

"Because I told you that I do."

"But how do I know you really mean it? How will I ever really know?"

"You're going to have to take my word for it."

"That's not good enough. I would have to know for sure. I would have to know for sure that you really forgive me."

"How?"

Michael removed his life jacket as he spoke. "I jump in. If you jump in after me, then I'll know."

"That is the dumbest thing I ever heard you say," said Freddie.

"It's the only way, the only way for me."

"Knock it off."

"I can't swim, but I wouldn't sink to the bottom right away. You are a strong swimmer—

"Mike, it's night."

"You have lights on the boat."

"Stop talking like this."

"It's the only way I'll know for sure."

"Mike—

Michael tossed his life jacket at Freddie and flipped backward into the water. Freddie sprung to his feet and rushed to turn on the boat's spotlight. He put it on the water. There, three feet from the boat, Michael thrashed in the water for his life. His hands clawed the surface, and every few seconds his head appeared as he choked and inhaled the sea. Freddie took off his life jacket, and looked down at his friend, at the horrible sight of a man battling for every breath he could steal. Freddie thrust his hand out toward him and was about to yell at Michael to take it, but then stopped. Freddie knelt in the boat watching Michael struggle for his life, steadily losing strength in his chest and arms. He pictured Lynn lying in those arms. Freddie withdrew his hand as the splashing sounds diminished, as the frequency with which Michael's head appeared above the water decreased until it sank below the water and did not resurface.

In the distance, Freddie could see other boats, clients of his, people he considered friends, but none like Michael. He knew he would never have a friend like Michael, and he sat in the boat looking for air bubbles to break on the surface until he could no longer see them.

DUMB

The road tried to tell me something
As I skipped along its path
Tumbling and turning
Burning and smeared
It peeled me like an egg
And fried me on the street
I laid down to die
Waiting for something that never came
Some last bit of wisdom
A last measure of salvation
I thought I heard the rattling
Of St. Peter's keys
But the keys were from the EMTs
And then from the mortician
And then from the grave digger
As he laid me in the hole
As dumb as I've ever been
And never to be any smarter
But that's what happens
When you've made yourself dumb
Actively, intentionally
With yet another bad call
By turning your eye from the road
For what seemed like a second

Lures

To see what's been going on
On other paths that maybe
You should've taken

SPREAD MY ASHES LIKE WE PLANNED

FIVE HUNDRED MILLION YEARS ago, at a place on the border of what is now Pennsylvania and New Jersey, the Delaware River cut through a ridge of the Appalachian Mountains to form a water gap. It was there that Nickels, Diggs, and Johnny Ballgame decided to start the tradition of an annual canoe trip.

"It's going to be great," said Diggs.

"I can't wait," said Nickels.

"I can't wait," said Johnny Ballgame.

They decided that they would drive to the Delaware Water Gap the third Friday of every August.

"We're going to drive to the Delaware Water Gap on the third Friday of every August," said Diggs.

"Sounds great," said Nickels.

"Sounds great," said Johnny Ballgame.

The first year they went, it rained.

"Too bad it's raining," said Diggs.

"Maybe it'll stop," said Nickels.

"It'll definitely stop," said Johnny Ballgame.

That weekend received a record amount of rain.

The three men made the best of it.

"Pass me that beer, Ballgame," said Diggs.

Ballgame passed Diggs a beer and then drank two himself. Johnny always drank twice the volume of the other two, and drank until he was blackout drunk. He taught the other two that blackout drunk is different than passed-out drunk.

Every canoe trip, someone would comment on how long it took to get there. Every year, someone would look at the darkening sky and place odds on the chance of rain. Every year, they would stop by the side of the road to take a picture of Johnny Ballgame saluting the billboard for Hickory Licks Rib Shack that showed a man eating ribs with BBQ sauce smeared all over his face and his hair on fire. Every year, they talked about the trip they wanted to take to Dublin. Every year, it poured down rain.

"It's going to rain."

"It always rains here."

"Why do we keep coming here?"

"It's tradition."

"Oh right."

One year, much like any other, Johnny Ballgame died.

Nickels and Diggs decided to carry on the tradition of the canoe trip, because "That's what Ballgame would have wanted."

Diggs and Nickels told everyone in town that they had decided to spread Johnny Ballgame's ashes around their camp site.

"We're going to spread Johnny Ballgame's ashes around our campsite," said Diggs. Everyone in town thought it was a wonderful idea.

On the third Friday of the next August, Diggs and Nickels set out for their usual campsite in the Delaware Water Gap with a coffee can that contained Johnny Ballgame's ashes.

"We have to make a few stops first," said Diggs.

"Where?" asked Nickels.

"Smackey Jack's," said Diggs, which was one of Ballgame's favorite bars.

"To toast Johnny?" asked Nickels.

"You got it," said Diggs.

They took their usual seats at the bar and engaged in breezy conversation with Stew the bartender. Stew served them their usual, a Pabst pounder and a shot of Jim Beam. They toasted Johnny before throwing back the shot and guzzling the beer until the cans were empty.

"Hey Stew?" asked Diggs.

"Yeah?"

"Can you put the ballgame on?"

"There's no ballgame on right now—

"BALLGAME!" yelled Diggs, and with that he threw a handful of Johnny Ballgame's ashes right in Stew's face. Diggs hopped off the barstool, grabbed Nickels by the front of his shirt, and dragged him out of the bar.

"Why did you do that?" asked Nickels.

"That's what Johnny wanted us to do."

Diggs explained to Nickels that Johnny left very clear instructions about what was to be done with his ashes.

"So we're not going canoeing?" asked Nickels.

"We are. But we have to do this first."

"Well, save some ashes for the river."

Diggs and Nickels visited ten of their favorite bars before driving to the Water Gap, and in each one, Diggs, and sometimes Nickels, threw Johnny Ballgame's ashes into the bartender's face.

On the road to the river, the weather turned, and Diggs put bets on the darkening sky.

When they came upon the Hickory Licks Rib Shack billboard, Nickels took a picture of the coffee can sitting next to the billboard of the man eating ribs with BBQ sauce smeared all over his face and his hair on fire.

From there they drove until they arrived at the canoe rental place. They talked about their trip to Dublin and how great it was going to be.

They placed their gear into the canoe and the sky opened up.

"Why do we keep coming here?" said Nickels. "It always rains."

"It's tradition," said Diggs.

"Right."

It poured down rain until they pushed the canoe ashore at their usual spot to set up camp.

Diggs told Nickels to build the fire since Johnny Ballgame did it in the past. Nickels started by getting one piece of wood at a time and carrying it from the woods to the fire pit. All of the wood was wet. Nickels went through a pack of matches trying to light it.

"Hey," Diggs said. "You keep doing the same thing over and over again and you can see it doesn't work. Are you stupid?"

"Do we really need a fire?" asked Nickels.

"We always have a fire," said Diggs.

"Right."

They never did start a fire, and later as they pounded beers in the dark, Nickels asked: "So do you think that what we did in those bars was wrong?"

"It's what Ballgame wanted," said Diggs. "He told us to shout his name and throw his ashes in the face of every bartender in every bar we used to go to, and that's what we did."

"I really miss him," said Nickels.

"Me too, Nicky. I really do."

"I wonder why he wanted us to do that. What does he have against bartenders? They gave him all those free drinks. They used to pour whiskey down his throat. Man, were they pissed at us."

"Ballgame was kinda weird sometimes," said Diggs. "Remember our last trip up here with him? That was really weird."

"Yeah, he wouldn't drink."

"Yeah. Weird."

"Yeah. You really gave him a hard time about that."

"Not that bad," said Diggs.

"No, you really rode him about it the whole weekend until he caved."

"You were riding him right along with me."

"But not like you."

"Didn't you say that him not drinking was like Superman not being able to fly?"

"I said that?" asked Nickels.

"You did."

ABOUT THE AUTHOR

John DiFelice was born in Philadelphia, Pennsylvania. His childhood was filled with hilarious adventures, colorful characters, and he's not allowed to write about any of it because his parents, similar to Holden Caulfield's, would have two conniptions apiece if he revealed anything remotely personal. Instead, he learned to make things up, which led to his love of writing fiction. This was, in fact, his third attempt to write this paragraph.

After writing a really bad, Gen-Xer, angst-ridden novel in his mid-twenties, he didn't write anything for a long time because he was so ashamed. That changed when he joined a sketch comedy troupe in Philadelphia and wrote sketches for an original monthly show. During that time he had two full-length plays produced off-Broad Street, and had a short story published in a collection called *South Philly Fiction* (Don Ron Books, 2013). His debut novel, *American Zeroes*, was published in July 2016, and for a time was #1 in the Kindle Store in the Satire category.

John lives in Philadelphia with his wife and son. He is working on his second novel, *Traffic Girl Wars*.

Made in the USA
Middletown, DE
15 June 2017